KIPPER & CO.
STRIKE AGAIN!

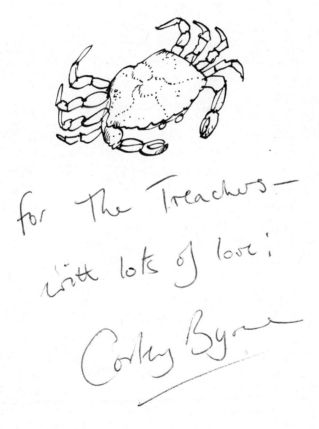

for The Treachers —
with lots of love;

Corky Byr...

First published in 1990
Text copyright © Corley Byrne, 1990
Illustrations copyright © Scoular Anderson, 1990

Printed in Great Britain
for J. M. Dent & Sons Ltd
91 Clapham High Street
London SW4 7TA

British Library Cataloguing in Publication Data
Byrne, Corley
  Kipper & Co. strike again.
  I. Title   II. Anderson, Scoular
  823'.914 [F]

ISBN 0–460–88028–4

KIPPER & CO. STRIKE AGAIN!

CORLEY BYRNE
Illustrated by Scoular Anderson

Dent Children's Books
LONDON

*For John and family
and Jane and family,
with thanks.*

Contents

1

Ninety-two Quid

THE school bleeper shrilled to signal the end of another day at Rexley Manor Comprehensive. Mr Foster, form tutor of 1B, raised his voice sharply to make himself heard above the sudden clamour of voices and outbreak of chair-scraping and desk-locker banging.

"Quietly, 1B – QUIETLY! Now," he went on as the noise subsided a little, "those of you who are interested in coming on the school holiday to Midwell Bay, show your parents the letters I've given you, and tell them to ... BE QUIET, MACKENZIE!"

A sturdy, ginger-haired, freckle-faced boy in the back row stopped in mid-yell and looked at Mr Foster with an expression of innocent surprise.

"Me, Sir? I *am* being quiet, sir," he protested. "I was only talking quietly to Andrew Quine."

Mr Foster closed his eyes, counted to ten, and calmed down. It was hometime. Christopher Mackenzie was going to be someone else's responsibility for a few hours.

"Just wait till you get outside before you start bellowing at each other, will you? Until that happy moment, SHUT UP! Right. The school holiday. Tell your parents that if you're coming, we shall need their cheques for ninety-two pounds by Monday at the latest. Now file out. QUIETLY!" he roared as the clamour, banging and scraping started again.

"Sir?"

Mr Foster looked down. Kipper Mackenzie and Andrew Quine stood in front of him. Andrew, a small, wiry boy with lank light-brown hair and rather protuberant ears, had been Kipper's best friend and constant partner in crime since their first sandpit fight in infant school. To this day, any disturbances in the classroom could generally be traced to these two. Next to Andrew were the other two members of the gang, the Chand twins, Rasheeda and Maya. Mr Foster could have told the twins apart quite easily even if Rasheeda hadn't worn her hair in an untidy ponytail and Maya didn't peer out from behind round, plastic spectacles, because Rasheeda, the younger and more wide-awake of the pair, was always the one who did the talking for both of them. She was doing it right now.

"Should be a good holiday, shouldn't it, sir? We're going to ask if we can go, sir. All of us."

"You coming, sir?" asked Mackenzie cheerfully.

"I am," agreed Mr Foster. "It's one of the many joys of being a first-form tutor. I get to accompany you rabble on holiday."

The four clattered outside, pushing and shoving each other through the door, talking loudly and excitedly. Mr Foster raised his eyes to the ceiling.

"And next year, I'm putting in for a sixth form," he muttered.

All the way home on the school bus, Kipper, Andrew and the twins discussed the holiday at the tops of their healthy young voices. Since Mr Foster had handed out the letters that morning, telling of a week's holiday in Mid-well Bay with swimming, canoeing, raft-building, beach-combing, two nights' camping under canvas and many other delights, they had been able to think or speak of little else.

"It'll be dead brilliant," Kipper prophesied, as they jumped down from the bus in their village of Rexley Green. "A whole week off school, camping and swimming and that, instead of doing work – can't be bad, can it?"

"Even if old Fossil-face is coming," Rasheeda reminded him.

"Yeah, well. He can't set us any maths on holiday, can he?" Kipper leapt on Andrew, hooked a foot around his ankle and tumbled them both to the ground.

Maya blinked at them anxiously as they scuffled and pummelled each other exuberantly.

"But Kipper, what if our parents say no?"

Kipper rose, dishevelled, and pushed his hair out of his eyes. "They won't," he said confidently. "Just keep telling 'em how educational it is. You'll see!"

He backed up, took a run at the hedge surrounding his front garden, leapt it, caught his foot on the top as usual and went sprawling in his mother's flowerbed, to the sarcastic cheers of his friends.

He jumped up and made a mock-rush at Andrew and the twins, who scattered, still giggling. Then he picked up the torn plastic carrier bag which carried his homework books from the rose bush in which it had landed, and sauntered round to the back door of his house, swinging the bag and whistling loudly.

When he entered the kitchen, he headed straight for the biscuit tin. His mother looked him up and down. The wrestling match with Andrew and the tumble in the flowerbed had added further mud and grass stains to those already collected on his uniform during an impromptu game of football on the school field at lunchtime.

"How *do* you do it?" she sighed. "How do you manage to return from school each day looking like you've just gone ten rounds with a mud-wrestler? . . . And wash your hands before you touch those biscuits."

"Too late," said Kipper through a mouthful. "I'll wash them now. Mum," he continued from the sink, "you'd like me to go on an educational holiday, wouldn't you?"

Mrs Mackenzie looked at the filthy marks on the tea towel on which Kipper had just dried his hands. "Who'd take you?" she asked.

Kipper explained that the school would. His mother scanned the letter which he produced from his school bag.

"Looks all right. Show your father," she said.

Kipper showed his father the letter as soon as he came home from work. Mr Mackenzie studied it and enquired just how educational this educational holiday was going to be. Kipper assured him they'd be being educated all the time.

"We'll be going round old houses and . . . and old castles, and stuff." He followed his father into the living room and took a flying leap on to the sofa. "And museums and . . . and nature reserves, and that . . . Think of the peace and quiet."

"I defy any nature reserve to be peaceful and quiet with

you lot rampaging through it," observed Mrs Mackenzie, coming in with a tray. Kipper filched another biscuit neatly from the tray as she passed.

"No, I meant the peace and quiet *here*, while I'm away being educated," he explained.

Mr Mackenzie thought of the peace and quiet. A smile spread across his face. Quickly, Kipper followed up his advantage.

"A whole week – and it's only ninety-two quid."

"Sold," said his parents together.

Kipper gave an exuberant whoop, sprang up and charged out to spread the good news.

He met the twins in the village street. From their wide, happy smiles he could tell that their parents had said yes too.

"Our dad wasn't sure *right off*," said Rasheeda, as usual getting in first and doing the talking for both of them, "but we kept saying it'd be good for our educations, and when he heard Mrs Tandy and Miss Lambe would be coming along to look after us girls, he said okay."

Kipper punched the air in triumph. "It's going to be *brilliant* with all us lot along . . ."

His voice faded. He had suddenly seen the small, wiry figure of Andrew trudging along the lane towards them, the picture of misery. His head was down, his shoulders were hunched up, and he was dragging the toes of his shoes through the gravel. He didn't even look up at his friends.

"I can't go," he muttered.

"What?" Kipper stared at him. "Why not?"

Andrew swallowed hard. "My dad said so. 'Cause of the sink."

Kipper groaned at the memory. Two weeks earlier, Andrew's grandmother had unwisely sent him a home chemistry set, in the hopes that it might foster in him a liking for science. To an extent, it had indeed done so;

for while both Kipper and Andrew showed only a moderate interest in supervised chemical experiments in the lab, being let loose on a chemistry set at home was a very different matter. They had set to with great enthusiasm in Andrew's kitchen, while his stepmother was out.

"They can't punish you again for that!" protested Kipper, outraged. "It wasn't even our fault! It didn't say on the box that if you mixed all those chemicals together they melted the enamel off sinks, did it? And we've already had our pocket money stopped for it ..." He almost choked with indignation. This was going too far.

But Andrew gulped and explained miserably that his father had promised him that this was not another punishment. It was just that the bill for the new sink unit had arrived that morning, and it was higher than they had expected.

"And now he's not going to have ninety quid left this month to pay for my holiday. He said he's sorry. So did my stepmum. It can't be helped, they said."

Kipper suddenly brightened. He saw a way out of the problem. Why couldn't Andrew's father pay *next* month? After all, the holiday itself wasn't till next month, so Andrew would still be paying for it about the time he went on it, wouldn't he?

Next day in school they tackled Mr Foster about it, but Mr Foster shook his head.

"Sorry, lads. Payment by next Monday at the latest. Those aren't my rules, they're the holiday company's."

"But that's not fair!" Rasheeda burst out, when they were safely outside.

Maya looked near to tears. "Kipper, can't we *do* something?"

Kipper was deep in thought. "Don't worry – we're going to," he muttered.

The idea of the holiday without Andrew was not to be contemplated even for a moment. Somehow, they HAD to fix it so that the whole gang could go.

All through lessons that day, Kipper's mind was racing. He formulated several wild schemes for raising money quickly, including hunting for treasure and robbing a bank. But they'd often hunted for treasure, and found none. The bank robbery was an idea that tempted him more . . . He fancied the thought of bursting into a bank with a stocking over his head, armed to the teeth and yelling, "Stick 'em up! Put the money in the bag!" . . .

"Christopher," cooed Mrs Tandy.

Kipper, who was driving his getaway car in a daring and brilliant high-speed car chase, hotly pursued by several police cars, gave a jump and blinked at her.

"What, Miss?"

"Are you gazing out of the window for inspiration, or are you just daydreaming?" she asked. But she said it with a smile.

Kipper liked Mrs Tandy; she was one of the more human of the teaching staff, in his opinion.

"Miss . . . if you wanted to raise a hundred pounds, and you needed it by Monday, how'd you go about it?"

Mrs Tandy laughed. "With the current state of *my* finances, I'd be lucky to raise a hundred *pence* by Monday. But I suppose I'd go down on my knees to my bank manager, and beg him for a loan. Why do you ask? What do you want a hundred pounds for?"

"Oh, nothing, really," said Kipper. "I was just wondering . . . Thanks, Miss."

A faint green light flickered in his eye. She had given him an idea.

After school, the Co. ignored the bus that would have taken them back to Rexley Green, and headed instead for the bank in the centre of Leatherham where Kipper knew his parents had their account.

Andrew's spirits were flagging. "Banks won't lend *us* money," he said gloomily.

"'*Course* they will. It's what they're there for, isn't it? To lend people money." Kipper pushed open the doors of the bank confidently. "Wait here," he instructed the others.

Two minutes later, he was ejected from the bank by two grinning bank clerks.

"Did you get the money?" asked Rasheeda.

Kipper glowered. "Flipping heck! Telling me I had to have an account with 'em before they'd lend me anything. I told 'em my dad did, *and* my mum, but they just laughed!" He rubbed his arm tenderly. "That bloke in there had a grip like a gorilla . . . I *bet* I'm bruised. And *laughing* at me!" His wounded pride was smarting. "I told 'em I'd start up an account with them when I start getting pocket money again if they'd lend me the ninety-two quid today . . . Well, I'm not now. They're *never* getting *my* money. *Huh*! That lot don't know what banks are *for*!"

He marched off down the street. Andrew followed dejectedly, trailing behind his three friends.

"He'll be doing lessons while we're away on the holiday. Can you imagine?" whispered Rasheeda. They shuddered at the thought.

"Look, we're not giving up yet," Kipper declared. "We've only tried the bank. There's tons of other ways to get money . . . And we've got all tomorrow and Sunday to do it."

"I can't do anything tomorrow," said Andrew hollowly. "They're taking me to the Sunshine Brothers' Amusement Park. I s'pose they think it'll make up for not going on the holiday."

Kipper frowned. He wasn't going to give up that easily . . .

That evening, a programme on TV gave him a brilliant idea. It was about the 1849 Gold Rush in America, and it showed exactly how men "panned" the rivers with big, flat sieves, finding tiny gold nuggets in amongst the mess which they had dredged up from the river bottom. Kipper leaned forward in his seat and watched attentively, much to his parents' gratification. It was seldom that Kipper paid any attention to a programme that seemed remotely educational.

When it was over, he slipped into the kitchen, appro-

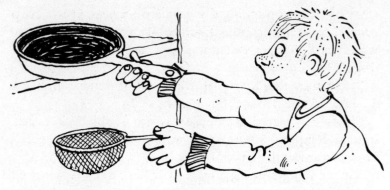

priated his mother's flour-sieve and frying-pan, and hid them in his bedroom.

Early next morning, he smuggled them out of the house. He met the twins, as prearranged, in the Co.'s favourite haunt, the wild woodland at the bottom of the Old Rectory garden. Rasheeda frowned when he explained his plan to them.

"What's panning for gold?" The twins had obviously not seen the programme.

"You just scrape the pan in the river, then you sieve the stuff and pick out the bits of gold. It's dead easy."

Maya blinked at the muddy stream that wound its way through the woodland. "Do you really think there's gold in there, Kipper?"

"'Course there is. Tons of it."

"Well, why's no one ever found any, then?" Rasheeda challenged him.

"'Cause no one's ever looked, have they?" said Kipper witheringly. "*You* ever seen anyone panning this river? Well, then. All the gold's still in there, isn't it? Makes sense. Come on! I'm having the frying-pan first."

They set to with a will, taking it in turns to dip the frying-pan into the stream bed, then tipping the resultant murky sludge into the sieve and searching eagerly through it. They found stones, sticks, mud, a caddis-fly, two water-boatmen and plenty of waterweed. They dislodged two rusty old tins, something that might once have been a crisp packet, several ring-pulls from drinks cans, and yet more waterweed. Kipper disentangled it and threw it aside in disgust.

"I bet they don't have all this *weed* in American rivers ... Hey! A stickleback! Give us the sieve!"

"Missed!" jeered Rasheeda, as the stickleback neatly evaded Kipper's swipe with the sieve and disappeared downstream with a flick of its tail.

Kipper slung some waterweed at her, and she smacked a handful of water at him. A fast and furious water-fight followed.

Eventually, soaked and laughing, they waded out of the water and decided to build a dam across the stream, for, as Kipper said, it would be a lot easier to see what you were panning for if the water was shallower.

They collected large stones and mud from the banks of the stream and set to work. Two hours later, they had built a dam across half the stream, and had three more water-fights and two weed-slinging contests. Rasheeda had loosened the handle of the frying-pan, Maya had jammed the sieve in the mud and torn its mesh, and Kipper had cut his finger on the jagged edge of a rusty can, but they had still not found so much as one small nugget of gold.

"Maybe we've got the wrong sort of rivers," suggested Maya.

Kipper, sucking his bleeding finger, nodded. The same thought had occurred to him. "Yeah, could be ... those old forty-niner blokes didn't keep finding tiddlers and coke cans. ... Well, I'm hungry. Let's go home for lunch, and carry on afterwards."

The twins agreed to this with enthusiasm.

When Kipper trudged into the kitchen, his mother took one look at his soaking clothes and soggy trainers, and groaned. "Hello, Swamp Man." Then her eyes widened.

"What's all the *blood*?"

Kipper looked at his shirt. "What blood? Oh, that. I cut my finger. There was this old can in the stream . . ."

He held up a grimy finger, the top half sucked clean, to show her.

"Oh, good grief," said his mother. "Get in the car, go on."

Protesting loudly, Kipper was driven to the hospital in Leatherham and propelled firmly into the casualty unit.

"I don't *need* it seeing to! It's only a small cut . . ."

"You need a tetanus jab, if nothing else. Now sit there while I fill in the form. Read a magazine, or something," his mother instructed him.

Kipper sighed and dropped into one of the chairs in the waiting-room. There were half a dozen old magazines on a low table nearby. He looked at them contemptuously. Women's magazines. Huh, you wouldn't catch him reading soppy drivel like that. Not on pain of *torture*.

A caption on the front cover of the top one caught his eye. "I FOUND A FORTUNE IN THE ATTIC!" it announced.

Kipper snatched it up and read the article eagerly. A woman, it transpired, had been hunting through her attic when she came upon an old vase which must have belonged to the previous owner of the house, now deceased. Although the vase was very ugly, the woman had decided to get it valued, and it had turned out to date from the eighteenth century, and to be worth over a thousand pounds . . .

Kipper whistled, causing a passing nurse to glare at him. A thousand quid – *Crikey!* Just for an ugly old vase! And his mother had loads of horrible old junk up in their attic . . .

The gleam of inspiration entered his eye again.

2

The Great Garage Sale

AN hour and a half later, Kipper joined the twins at the stream. They looked fed up and bored.

"Where've you been?" demanded Rasheeda. "We couldn't pan for gold without the pan, and we've been waiting *hours* and *hours* . . ."

Kipper dismissed her protests with a wave of his newly bandaged hand. "I've been up the hospital getting stitches and a jab, and we're not panning for gold any more anyway," he declared. "I've got a much better idea. Come on!"

They followed him at a run to his house. Kipper explained on the way.

Eagerly they swarmed up the stepladder to the attic. There was a box full of junk by the skylight; Kipper dived on it triumphantly.

"This is stuff she puts aside for Boot Fairs and things . . . Hey, look at *this*!"

He held up an old Toby jug. It had a hideous, leering expression and was badly chipped.

"This is old. I bet *this* is worth a bit!"

"Here's a watch!" said Rasheeda. "And the bottom of a lamp-thingy . . ."

"And a sort of a toast-rack . . ."

"And two eggcups shaped like chickens . . . We've had those for hundreds of years, so they've *got* to be old. Come on! There's an antiques shop in the village. Let's take 'em there."

Proudly they staggered down the High Street with the

box. The proprietor of the antiques shop gave them a suspicious look as they entered.

"Don't you come in here wasting my time," he growled.

"We're not," said Kipper, dumping the box on the counter. "We're giving you first chance of buying these valuable antiques from us."

He tipped the box's contents on to the counter. The proprietor's face grew purple. He spluttered. He seemed to have lost his voice.

Kipper held up the Toby jug. "This one alone's probably worth nearly a thousand . . . well, that's what old vases are worth, aren't they? But we'll let you have it for a lot less," he added kindly. "And see this watch? It's antique. Well, it's got hands and it's not digital, so it's pretty old, and it almost works, too . . ."

"And we only want ninety-two pounds for the lot," put in Rasheeda.

The proprietor still had not found his voice, but he didn't seem to need it. With a deft movement he swept the con-

tents back into the box, deposited it in Kipper's arms and propelled him firmly out of the shop. Then he returned to push the twins out, and slammed and bolted the door behind them.

"Well, that's nice!" snorted Rasheeda. "Not even speaking to us ... oh, very nice, I *must* say!"

Kipper frowned – and then his countenance lightened again. He knew that his mother would be out all afternoon; she had gone to buy a new pair of shoes, and she generally went to every shoe-shop in Leatherham at least twice before she decided on anything. And his father was out for the whole day, too, fishing.

"We'll sell this stuff ourselves. We'll have a Garage Sale, in my garage. They make a ton of money! You two go and see what *you* can find to sell, and then come to my place."

They scattered, the twins heading eagerly for the small supermarket which their father ran.

Half an hour later, they arrived at Kipper's house lugging a carrier bag between them. Kipper had dragged the garden table round to the front and set it up before the open garage. Stuck to it was a sign written in red felt-tip pen on the torn-off top of the cardboard box. It read:

GARIJ SALE TODAY LOTS OF BARGANS,
REAL ANTEEKS!

Kipper was arranging the contents of the box on the table. The twins turned out their bag. There was a loaf of very mouldy bread, two big bags of self-raising flour, some potatoes that had sprouted, some bruised apples, an orange and a few broken biscuits.

"I know they're not antiques," said Maya, "but they're all past their sell-by dates, so my dad doesn't want them. And those bags of flour've split, and the orange is a bit squishy underneath, and they're all things that can raise money for Andrew," she added shyly.

Kipper nodded. "All right. Bung 'em on the stall. We'll be getting our first customer any time now, I bet you."

Maya pointed down the street. Kipper turned and grimaced as he saw a thin, long-faced boy approaching.

Rasheeda groaned. "Oh, not *him* ... not old Parsnip-features!"

Quentin Parslow was the Co.'s biggest foe from school. Already that week he had landed Kipper and Andrew in trouble three times by telling on them – twice for having paper-pellet fights during Maths, and once for sellotaping the legs of his chair to his desk in revenge for having "told".

Kipper gave him a narrow-eyed glare. "What do *you* want?"

"You're breaking the law," said Quentin Parslow in his shrill voice. "You're not allowed to have sales and things without permission. I'll *tell* on you." He looked at the contents of the table and sneered. "Anyway, it's all trash you're selling. Just a load of old junk."

"Oh, it is, is it? Just shows what *you* know," retorted Rasheeda. "They're all antiques, this lot."

Quentin Parslow jeered. "Yeah? The oldest thing on this table's that loaf of bread. It's all mouldy."

"Mouldy!" Kipper shook his head pityingly. "He thinks it's *mouldy*! Listen, it's ... it's green wholemeal bread, mate. You'd pay a quid for that up the health shop. *We're* selling it for tenpence."

Quentin Parslow blinked at the loaf uncertainly; Kip-

26

per's tone held conviction. "Anyway," he rallied, moving back on to safer ground, "you're still breaking the law. You need *permission* for garage sales, I'm telling you."

"We've got it," said Kipper, without blushing.

"So get lost, Parsley-face," added Rasheeda.

Quentin Parslow kicked out slyly at the leg of the table, and the table jerked and almost collapsed. The twins dived to save it, and Kipper sprang at Quentin Parslow, who turned and fled, squealing. "Don't you touch me . . . I'll *tell*!"

Kipper grabbed a sprouting potato off the stall, pursued Quentin to the end of the road and flung the potato with unerring aim. Quentin Parslow's howl floated back as Kipper returned, dusting his hands off.

"And that's got rid of *him*. Now I bet we'll get some proper customers along soon."

They waited. Several cars passed but none stopped, although many of the drivers seemed to be grinning about something. Then three boys approached. Kipper recognised them; they had been in the year below him at Rexley Green Primary School.

One of the boys, a lad with curly hair and protruding teeth, pointed. "How much d'you want for that?"

Kipper picked up the Toby jug. "Good choice. It's an antique. Worth hundreds of pounds, but we're letting it go for five – "

"Not that!" said the boy scornfully. "*That*!" and he pointed again.

Kipper followed the direction of his finger into the garage, and his eyebrows shot up.

"My dad's bike? Give over, that's not for sale!"

"'Course it is. It's in the garage, isn't it? And this is a Garage Sale. You've got to sell us anything in the garage. I'll give you two quid for it."

Kipper stood open-mouthed as the boys swarmed past him into the garage. He grabbed the garden hose from

27

one, and the watering-can from another, and turfed them out. Then he returned for the curly-haired one, who dodged away from him and sprinted up the road.

"Yah – flipping *cheats*!" the boy yelled. "You don't know how to have a proper Garage Sale . . ."

Kipper took a couple of steps towards him and the boy vanished around the corner.

Suddenly there was a piercing whistle and a series of derisive shouts behind them. Kipper turned.

A tall, stocky, pugnacious-looking boy with a spotty face was leering at him. It was Willis of form 2X, with a couple of the moronic thugs who went around with him – and that sneaky little Quentin Parslow, who was jigging up and down, squeaking eagerly.

"See, Willis? I *told* you what he was doing!"

Kipper almost groaned. The appearance of Willis couldn't mean anything but trouble.

"Scrape off, Willis, unless you've come to buy something."

"Nah," said Willis, grinning. "We're not here to buy – we're here to *give* you something. We thought you'd like some more rotten veggies for your stall . . ."

Something soggy and wet and juicy splattered all over Kipper's T-shirt.

"Have a tomato," grinned Willis.

Suddenly all the thugs were throwing tomatoes, from bags which they produced from behind their backs. One tomato hit Rasheeda on the ear, a second smacked Kipper's neck, and he felt it slide down the inside of his shirt. He sprang for the sprouting potatoes and began buzzing them at Willis. Rasheeda followed suit, slinging potatoes with a will. She scored a direct hit on Quentin Parslow's bony nose with the squishy orange, and he retreated, holding his nose and yelling.

"CHARGE 'EM!" bellowed Willis.

They charged, barging Rasheeda aside; then they grabbed the table and heaved, upending it. The Toby jug slid off and shattered on the ground. One of the bags of self-raising flour burst. Kipper, his face streaming with tomato juice and pips, scooped up a handful of the flour and pushed it into Willis's face.

At this stage of the fight, Maya, who had been in the garage, snatched up the watering-can and disappeared round the side of the garage with it. No one noticed her go. Willis was roaring and spluttering, clawing flour out of his eyes and mouth. One of his moronic mates had dumped a giant handful of flour over Kipper in retaliation, but this didn't stop Kipper noticing that one of the bags of flour was still whole . . .

He pounced on it. A huge flour bomb was exactly what he needed at this stage of the battle.

"Look out!" Willis yelled suddenly. His gang scattered.

Kipper threw the flour bomb just as his father's car turned into the driveway.

It burst on the gleaming bonnet of the car, exploded in a thick cloud, and rained gently down on Mr Mackenzie through the open sun-roof.

Kipper stood frozen with horror. Mr Mackenzie got out of the car slowly, shaking flour out of his hair and dusting off his shoulders. He appeared to be breathing very slowly and deeply, and counting to himself.

"You'll clean this car, Christopher," he said, levelly, and Kipper gulped at the use of his full name – that always meant trouble. "I realise that that flour wasn't meant for me, but all the same you will scrub the car, my lad, inside and out, until not one grain of flour remains, or I shall – UURRRGGH!"

He broke off with an ear-splitting yell as a deluge of icy-cold water hit him and the car with a loud, wet smack.

"Take *that*!" panted Maya. "You big bully . . ."

She stopped. Her eyes widened behind her spectacles. There was a moment's deep silence, then Rasheeda said, "Ooh, heck," and the twins turned and scuttled off.

Kipper would have followed them, but his father, who had recovered the use of his limbs after the shock of the freezing water, shot out a hand and grabbed him by the arm.

"Now *this*," he said between his teeth, "I want an explanation for, sunshine. And it had better be a flaming *good* one!"

Kipper gulped again, and started trying to explain about the Garage Sale and Willis's attack, but Mr Mackenzie, still dripping, was staring past him into the garage.

"Wait a minute! What Garage Sale? And WHERE'S MY BIKE?"

Kipper spun round and stared. The bicycle was gone. In its place, on the floor, were two pound coins . . .

Two eventful hours later, Kipper met the twins in their woodland retreat. He was rubbing his ear.

"There's s'posed to be laws against hitting kids, but *my* dad hasn't heard of 'em!" he complained bitterly. "Crikey, you should've *heard* him just now . . . I got his rotten bike back for him, didn't I? Cost me my new penknife, too, as well as the two quid, to get it back off those kids, when all I really wanted to do was murder 'em for sneaking in and nicking it like that . . . It wasn't *my* fault they'd bent its flipping back wheel, was it?"

"How?" asked Rasheeda.

Kipper glowered. "Doing wheelies on it. I could've *told* 'em that sort of bike doesn't do wheelies. I know, I've tried it. Flipping heck! My dad didn't half kill me when he saw it! *And* my mum blew her top. Just because she found that sieve and the frying-pan we'd used . . . Well, I can't help it if they make sieves that tear and frying-pans with handles that drop off soon as you look at them, can I? I'm not going to have any pocket money till I'm twenty the way *they* carry on!"

The twins murmured sympathetically.

"Well, we've blown it," said Kipper glumly, sitting down on a fallen tree-trunk and burying his chin in his hands. "We'll *never* get that money for Andrew now. My mum's nicked all her junk back and thrown the rest in the bin, so we've got nothing left to sell anyway. We've blown it."

Just then they heard a familiar, cheery whistle, and Andrew came bounding energetically through the wood to join them. He looked remarkably happy for someone who faced the grim prospect of doing a week's schoolwork while his friends were away on a holiday.

"Hey!" he greeted them. "The Sunshine Brothers' Park is brilliant. They've got this dead good ride. You go upside down about eight times on it. I had five goes. My dad got sick ..." He broke off, seeing his friends' gloomy expressions. "Crikey, you lot look a bit sick and all. What's up?"

"We *are* sick," said Rasheeda. "Sick of mucking it up every time we try and raise the money for you to come on this holiday."

Andrew clicked his fingers. "Hey, I knew there was something I wanted to tell you! I'm coming. My gran's paying for it!"

The twins squealed. Kipper jumped up and punched Andrew in celebration, a wide grin on his freckled face. "Mega! Tell you just now, did she?"

"No, she rang first thing this morning. Soon as my step-mum told her I couldn't go, she said she'd pay. She reckoned as it was her that gave me the chemistry set in the first place, she'd . . ." Andrew blinked at his friends. "Why are you all looking at me like that?"

Kipper broke the silence that had suddenly fallen. "You've known . . . since *this morning*?" he asked slowly.

"Why didn't you tell us?" gasped Rasheeda.

"I *am*, aren't I? I bet you're glad I'm coming. I bet . . . *hey*!"

Three pairs of hands had grabbed him.

He skidded down the bank, and landed with a splash in the stream.

3

The Cavemen Club

THREE weeks later, the day of departure arrived. At nine o'clock on Saturday morning, a coach turned up at the school gates and Mr Foster, Mrs Tandy and Miss Lambe shepherded thirty-two excited first-formers aboard.

Kipper and Andrew stampeded for the back seat, and got there first, ahead of Quentin Parslow, who squealed loudly and informed Mr Foster that they had trodden on his toes (which was true) and pulled him and Nigel Bailey off the back seat (which was not). Mr Foster made them give up the back seat to Quentin Parslow and Nigel Bailey, and Quentin Parslow pulled a triumphant face at them as he took it.

Kipper waited until the coach was on its way and then, under cover of the singsong Miss Lambe was trying to start up, he quietly extracted a can of cola from his backpack, shook it up thoroughly, directed it at Quentin Parslow and tugged back the ring-pull top. It was right on target.

Quentin Parslow's howl was echoed by Mr Foster's roar as he descended on Kipper, took him by one shoulder and Andrew by the other, and marched them up the coach to sit one beside him and one beside Mrs Tandy, leaving Quentin Parslow dripping with cola.

"One more move out of either of you . . ." he threatened.

The rest of the long journey was going to be pretty boring, Kipper could tell. You couldn't even enjoy yourself pulling horrendous faces at people in cars, not with old

Fossil-face right beside you.

Presently, Mrs Tandy took pity on Kipper's glowering, frozen expression of boredom. She took a brochure out of her bag.

"Here, Christopher. You might like to read a little more about where we're going."

Kipper accepted it with an inward groan. Still, it was probably better than sitting staring at the back of the driver's head all the way. He opened the brochure listlessly.

The information about the hostel in which they were to be staying did not interest him, but the next page did.

"The main beach at Midwell Bay," it informed him, "is known as Smugglers' Cliffs. Legend has it that in the eighteenth and nineteenth centuries gangs of smugglers operated very successfully in this area, smuggling contraband casks of rum, French brandy, and lace ..."

Kipper snorted. Brandy! Lace! Who'd bother to smuggle stuff like that? Now he'd recently seen a film about a gang of children who had become involved in an adventure with some modern-day smugglers. These smugglers had been smuggling gold and jewels, the proceeds of a robbery, *out* of the country. Such things were *worth* smuggling, in Kipper's opinion. They'd been very clever, hiding the goods in a cave under some marker stones, waiting until dead of night, then digging them up again and smuggling them out of the country in a sailing boat, without lights, so that the police couldn't see or hear them. Of course, the gang of children had caught them in the end. It had been an exciting film.

Kipper settled back in his seat, a faraway look in his eyes. He was "Fingers" Mackenzie, notorious criminal, planning his next escapade, smuggling gold out of the country under the very noses of the police. He was the young hero of the film, leading his gang in a bold and daring raid to trap the smugglers . . .

The countryside and the journey passed him by unnoticed. Before he realised it, the coach was pulling into the Sea View hostel.

Mr Foster called the first-formers back as they spilled eagerly off the coach.

"Wait! Now when told your room number, you will go there, unpack, and change into shorts for this afternoon's outing to the beach. You will then come to the dining-hall, which I will show you as we go in for lunch. Right, line up and get your room numbers!"

In a few minutes Kipper and Andrew were in their room, which they were sharing with two boys from form 1J. They "unpacked" by the simple method of turning the contents of their backpacks out on to their beds; they changed into their shorts, and engaged in a brief but vigorous pillow-fight to work off all the energy which they had had to stifle during their two-and-a-half hours on the coach. Then they charged down to the dining-hall and tucked into sausages, chips and peas, followed by double-sized portions of strawberry, chocolate and vanilla ice-cream. This holiday was going to be all right, Kipper decided, halfway through his second helping.

Lunch over, they set out for the beach, Mr Foster leading the exuberant, noisy group, Miss Lambe in the middle, trying to keep them in pairs, and Mrs Tandy at the rear, to ensure that any stragglers kept up. It was a short walk to the top of the cliffs, and a long clatter down a couple of hundred wooden steps to the beach itself.

The tide was out; the sea looked like a silvery strip in the distance, far away across the dark, wet sand. Mr Foster shot out a hand to grab Kipper by the shoulder.

"Just a minute! Before we start. *No one* is to attempt to swim here. The tide may be out, but I'm told it comes in very fast, and there are warnings about the strong currents in this area. The hostel has a swimming-pool; we'll go swimming there when we get back. You are *not* to go wandering off, or clambering about on the cliffs. Are you all listening? The purpose of this visit is to learn something about the fascinating shorelife you can see around you." He started to hand out worksheets. "You will find all manner of strange and wonderful beasties lurking about under rocks – and for once I'm not talking about Mackenzie."

A loud and derisive laugh went up, and Andrew shoved Kipper, who grinned. When old Fossil-face started making grotty jokes, at least it meant he was in a good mood.

Kipper looked around. This was a brilliant place. The cliffs towered overhead, running along the beach in a jagged line and forming lots of little private inlets and bays. It shouldn't be too hard to get into one of those, where no one would have a clear view of what you were doing . . . the pools of water all over the dark, sludgy wet sand looked inviting, too.

He scrunched up his worksheet and stuffed it into his shorts' pocket.

"Come on," he challenged Andrew and the twins, "race you to the water!"

They charged for the nearest pool, kicked off their shoes and leapt in. Soon their arms and legs were splattered with streaks of the sludgy sand. They chased each other with long, slimy strands of seaweed. They dug marks in the sand with their heels, and watched them quickly fill in and disappear. Kipper found a big crab and tried to pick it up, but it scrabbled furiously with all of its eight legs and sank sideways into the sand, holding its pincers up warningly.

Maya, who as usual was the only one conscientiously doing her worksheet, solemnly ticked off shore-crab.

"It says we've got to look on rocks for barnacles and stuff next."

Rasheeda pointed to a long promontory of rocks a little way ahead, which jutted out into the sea like a long, thin, pointing finger, forming a natural jetty.

"No one's looking on those rocks. Come on!"

They sprinted to the rocks, and swarmed over them.

"See who can catch a crab first," Kipper challenged them. "Bet it won't be as massive as the one I just . . ."

His voice died away. He stared into the next bay.

There, a short way up the cliff face, was a cave. A mysterious, dark entrance beckoned to them.

Kipper's eyes shone. He whistled softly, remembering the brochure. A cave! The perfect place for smugglers to hide contraband!

He glanced back over his shoulder. Mr Foster and the other teachers were busy looking into rockpools, surrounded by the other twenty-eight first-formers. Kipper signalled to the Co. to follow, then jumped down off the rocks and hurried towards the cave.

He paused to check that he was hidden from the teachers' view by the jutting cliffs, then he began to climb. It was a fairly easy scramble, over loose stones and shells at first, and there were footholds and handholds in the chalky cliff-side. In less than a minute Kipper was in the mouth of the cave.

He peered in and whistled again, then clapped a hand to his mouth as the sound of his whistle echoed hollowly back at him. He turned and waved excitedly to the others, who were clambering up to join him inside the cave.

Even in the dim light, they could see that his eyes were shining with excitement.

"What about this, then? It's mega-brilliant!"

The cave was small and damp-walled; its floor was dry, with powdery-white sand. A few stones and lumps of chalk lay scattered about. Maya shivered. Kipper's voice had sounded eery, reverberating around the small chamber.

"It's creepy," she whispered.

"It's perfect," said Kipper with confidence. "You know what this bay is called? Smugglers' Cliffs, that's what!"

"So?" Rasheeda was lost.

"So this is just the sort of cave they'd have hidden their stolen stuff in, isn't it!"

"Why?" asked Rasheeda.

Kipper gave her an exasperated look. "Because that's what they did, you dozo!"

"They'd have had to be pretty small smugglers," muttered Andrew, rubbing his head, which he had just banged for the second time on the cave roof.

"Well, that's why it's the perfect cave for 'em to use, isn't it? The police would think it was too small for 'em to get into and hide stuff, so they wouldn't bother looking in it . . . *Crikey*!" Kipper's voice almost cracked with excitement. He pointed into a corner, " *Look*! See that?"

They looked. In one corner, against the wall, was a pile of flat, white stones.

They blinked. "So?" asked Rasheeda again.

"Don't you get it? It's a mark! A smuggler's mark! They did that in this film I saw. They buried the treasure under a special pile of stones, and put the stones there to remind 'em where they'd hidden it for when they came back to dig it up! Well, do you see any stones exactly like those anywhere else in this cave?"

They didn't. The stones were flat, white and smooth, and all much the same size. They looked as if someone had spent a lot of time and care in selecting them.

"Crikey!" said Andrew hoarsely.

Kipper knelt down and had started to drag the stones aside when suddenly a deep, angry voice boomed round the cave, shattering the silence.

"MACKENZIE!"

Maya squealed in fright. Kipper dropped the stone he was holding.

"COME OUT HERE, ALL FOUR OF YOU!"

"Oh, heck," muttered Kipper.

Mr Foster was standing at the mouth of the cave as they trooped out.

"Yes, I thought so. Can't obey orders for ten minutes, can you! What did I tell you about not going clambering over the cliffs?"

"But it's dead good in there, sir. We've found . . ."

"Be QUIET! It's a good job someone spotted you climbing up here, or we would probably have called the coastguard out by now to start looking for you! You girls, get back to Mrs Tandy and *you* two," he took Kipper and Andrew by an arm each, "stay *right* beside *me*!"

As they trudged back to join the others, Kipper glanced at Quentin Parslow and Nigel Bailey. The pair of them were smirking broadly, and it dawned on Kipper that he could guess exactly *who* had spotted them climbing up to the cave. That slimy pair of sneaks must have followed them, and told on them.

Well, Fossil-face can't watch me all afternoon, he thought. Just wait. First chance I get, I'll search for another nice, big shore-crab.

Meantime, he decided to work out a way to get back to the cave and have another go at digging up the treasure.

By the time the group returned to the hostel three hours later, however, Kipper had still not managed to slip away and get back to the cave. His only moment of satisfaction that afternoon had come when Mr Foster had looked the other way just long enough to give him the chance to thrust a crab under Quentin Parslow's long, bony nose. When Quentin Parslow had run, screaming with fright, Kipper had turned his most innocent expression full on Mr Foster, and explained that he'd only been *showing* the crab to Quentin, and thought he'd have been *interested*.

Mr Foster contented himself with a low growl. The boy obviously thought himself safe because there were no detentions on holiday. Well, he had a surprise coming.

Back at the hostel, Mr Foster collected up all the work-sheets, except for two grimy, crumpled offerings. These he handed back to their authors, Kipper and Andrew, along with two clean new sheets, and informed them that after a drink of orange juice, everybody else would be going swimming in the hostel pool.

"You two, however, will not be joining us until you have handed in neat, clean copies of these filthy worksheets. Got that?"

Andrew's jaw dropped at the unfairness of making them do extra work on holiday, but Kipper kept his expression blank as he accepted his sheet. A small light gleamed in his eye.

"Yes, sir," he promised. "We'll stay in our room till it's done, sir."

"You'll stay in the common room," Mr Foster corrected him. "There's a table in there for you to work at, and I shall be coming back every few minutes to check up on you, so *don't* try bunking off."

Kipper crossed his fingers behind his back, said "Oh, *no, sir*," and closed one eye in a wink at Andrew. This was even better. The common room was on the ground floor.

He just had time to explain his plan to the twins while they were lining up for orange juice. Then Mr Foster

shepherded Kipper and Andrew into the common room and settled them down with their worksheets. He warned them again that he would be back to check up on them, and left them. Kipper counted up to thirty, then jumped up and scrambled out of the open window, Andrew close behind him.

From behind the hostel, they could hear shouts and laughter and splashes coming from the pool. They grinned at each other and sprinted for the path leading to the cliff top.

"We share whatever we find with the twins," Kipper suggested as they clattered down the wooden steps to the beach. "They *were* there when we found it – well, almost found it the first time."

Andrew agreed. It went without saying.

The tide was still several metres out as they raced over the sand, clambered over the rocky outcrop, and climbed eagerly up to the cave.

The sand under the flat white stones was dry and hard-packed. Kipper and Andrew each took a stone and began to dig, chipping away at the floor and scraping away the sand. They worked on for several minutes, until they had scraped a small hole about ten centimetres deep.

Then Andrew sat back on his heels, dropped his stone and glanced towards the cave entrance.

"Old Fossil-face'll have found us missing by now . . ."

Kipper gave him a stern look. "You what?"

43

"Well, we don't know there's anything *really* buried here," Andrew defended himself somewhat shamefacedly.

"What do you think we came back here for? To play sandcastles?"

But Andrew was getting uneasy. After all, this smugglers bit *was* just a game . . . and by now old Fossil-face was sure to have checked up on them.

"We'll get murdered," he muttered.

"All right," said Kipper witheringly. "You go back. Go on, you go back to the hostel, and I'm flipping well keeping your share of the treasure."

Andrew sighed, picked up his stone again and started to dig. Suddenly he jumped. His stone, instead of thudding into sand, had clanged on something hard. Something *very* hard, and metallic . . .

"There's something here!" he yelled.

Kipper whooped exultantly. "What did I tell you? Come on!"

They dug furiously, with renewed effort. Sand flew everywhere.

Soon the shape of the treasure became apparent. It was a round rusty tin of generous size. The boys dug and scrabbled eagerly until they could drag it out of the hole.

Reverently Kipper held it up, and shook it. "It's heavy!" His voice was hoarse with excitement. "And it rattles . . . there's something in here, all right!"

"Open it!" cried Andrew.

Kipper was already trying to do just that. He gasped in frustration as his fingers slipped on the lid.

"It's wedged. It's rusted on solid!"

They both tried tugging at it, but to no avail. So they turned it upside down, and used the stones to chip away at the edge of the lid. Soon Kipper gave a little cry. "It's coming!"

With one final bang, the lid was off, and the contents of the tin tumbled out into the sand.

Kipper and Andrew stared at them, open-mouthed.

There was a yellowed envelope, an old exercise-book, its once-red cover faded pink with age, a very rusty pen-knife with a broken blade, some coins, and a folded wodge of yellow-brown newsprint paper. Kipper picked this up.

"It's a newspaper ... No, it's not! It's a BEANO! Crikey, it's ancient. It's got ... 1954 on it. August, 1954!"

Andrew had opened the envelope. Very carefully, he pulled out a faded black-and-white photograph. The picture showed a group of five boys, aged between perhaps eight and eleven. They wore baggy short trousers down to their knees, and socks falling round their ankles. They were standing at the base of the cliff, with the cave above them, and they were all pulling faces at the camera. On the back of the photo was written "US – THE CAVE-MEN CLUB – TAKEN BY ME, ERIC – ORGUST 1954 AND BERRIED FOR HISTRY. DETH TO TRAITORS!"

Kipper took the photo, and whistled. "A cave'd make a *brilliant* gang hideout," he said enviously.

He opened the exercise-book in the hope of learning more about the Cavemen, but to his disappointment, anything that had been written there had been written in pencil, and it was now far too faded to be discernible. He picked up one of the coins.

"What's this?"

"An old halfpenny," said Andrew. "I've seen those before. My dad collects old coins ..." He paused, and cocked his head to one side suddenly. "Listen! Hear that?"

"What?"

"That – the sea-noise. It's got louder."

They went to the entrance of the cave and looked out.

Below them, the sea was just beginning to lap gently at the very foot of the cliffs.

4

Air–Sea Rescue

THE boys' eyes widened. "It wasn't this far in just now!" gasped Andrew.

"It's coming in flipping fast." Kipper began stuffing the contents back into the tin. "Come on, we'd better get back anyway. Old Fossil-face won't be too mad at us when he sees what we've found, I'll bet."

Andrew snorted. He had a feeling old Fossil-face would murder them.

They slithered down the last few feet of the cliff face and jumped into the water. It barely reached over their shoes. Keeping close in to the cliffs, they edged out round the headland and scrambled up on to the promontory of rocks.

They were about to jump down the other side into the water, when they heard a shout.

"Hoi! You lads!"

They turned, to see a man hailing them from a small fishing boat, which was bobbing up and down a short way out to sea.

"What?" yelled Kipper.

"Don't jump down the other side of those rocks, son! Tide's not at its highest yet, but the undercurrent there is still bad. If it doesn't smash you on the rocks, it'll drag you out to France!"

Kipper looked down at the water, puzzled. It didn't look that deep, or that bad.

"So what do we do?"

In answer, one of the fishermen began to manoeuvre

the boat close to the end of the rocky promontory, while
the other waved his arms in an invitation. The two boys
were quick to accept. They made their way along the rocks
carefully, remembering what the man had said, and each
in turn took the hand of the younger of the two fishermen,
who helped them to jump aboard the bobbing boat.

"Two stowaways safely aboard, Bill," he reported to
the older man.

"You're in luck," the one named Bill informed them,
as the boat headed out to sea. "Ten minutes later, we
wouldn't have been able to get near you, the currents would
have been that bad. We'd have had to call the coastguard
to send out an Air Sea Rescue helicopter!"

Just for a moment, Kipper experienced a twinge of
regret. Only a few more minutes in the cave, and they
could have been having a helicopter ride . . . Then he looked
around the boat, and his feelings changed. This was, after
all, the first time he'd ever been on a real fishing boat.
It smelt like one, too. It was brilliant.

He looked at the piles of nets on the damp floor of the
boat. "What do you catch with those?"

"Cod, mostly," said Bill. "Haddock . . . depends what's about, eh, Dave. Tell you what, son, you can have a go with 'em on the way back if you like."

Kipper and Andrew stared at each other in delight, then Kipper dropped the Cavemen tin and they dived to pick up the heavy wet nets.

Neither of them saw the irate figure running along the top of the cliffs, towards the steps.

Mr Foster had meant to go and check up on Kipper and Andrew after ten minutes, but just as he was going to leave the swimming-pool, Rasheeda had suddenly slipped in a puddle of water on the pool's edge and fallen into the shallow end with a loud shriek. She emerged close to tears, holding her right knee and complaining that she'd hit it on the bottom and it really hurt.

Rasheeda, limping heavily, was helped to her room by Mrs Tandy. Maya hid a smile. It had worked perfectly. Now Mr Foster was the only teacher left on duty at the pool, because Miss Lambe, who was prone to headaches, had gone to lie down for half an hour. And if Mr Foster was the only one at the pool, it meant he'd have to stay there. This would buy the boys a bit more time.

It was nearly ten minutes before Mrs Tandy got back. Rasheeda believed in playing a part to the full, and when her knee had refused to swell up or look injured, she had complained about her elbow, her shoulder and one of her big toes too. It was only when nothing looked discoloured or swollen that Mrs Tandy told Rasheeda she'd probably survive, left her lying on her bed, and went back to the pool.

Relieved of his duty, Mr Foster went to the common room at once.

It was empty.

Swearing under his breath, he began to search the hostel, checking first in the boys' room, then in the teachers' common room where the biggest colour television was, then in all the other rooms.

Suddenly he realised where they would be. That cave. Ten to one they had gone back there, just because they knew it was out of bounds.

Grimly he set off down to the beach at a brisk pace. At the top of the cliffs, he stopped and peered over. The tide was high, slapping at the foot of the cliffs. All that was visible of the beach was a short strip of rocks stretching out to sea. There was no sign of the boys, nothing but a small fishing boat in the distance.

Mr Foster could not see the cave from where he was. He tried shouting, "MACKENZIE! QUINE!" but no answering voices reached him. Well, even if it meant getting wet, he would have to go down there and check that cave. He was absolutely certain now that that was where those wretched boys would be.

He took the wooden steps three at a time, paused at the bottom to remove his shoes, and then, shoes in hand, gritted his teeth and stepped into the cold, swirling water. He waded out towards the rocks, knowing he would have to climb over them to reach the little bay where the cave was.

49

Suddenly the water got deeper. It was up to his calves, then his knees. He waded on.

Just as he reached the rocks, the tide suddenly sucked him off his feet. He toppled into the water with a yell, and tried to grasp the rocks to haul himself back to a standing position, but now that the undercurrent had got him, it wasn't going to release him. Slowly it tugged at him, dragging him out to deeper water, and within moments he was out of his depth.

He grabbed on to a rock as the waves banged him painfully against it, and using all his strength managed to haul himself out of the water on to the rock. A big wave broke over it, trying to drag him back in again.

Mr Foster backed away along the rocks towards the cliffs. Strong swimmer as he was, he knew better than to go back in the water now that he had experienced the undertow.

But he had to get off those rocks. He had to find the two missing boys . . . he shuddered at the thought of what might have happened to them.

He began to shout and wave his arms, but the one boat that had been around was now a speck on the horizon.

Aboard the boat, meanwhile, Kipper and Andrew were having the time of their lives. Dave and Bill had let each of them have a go at steering the boat, and had even thrown out one of the nets to show them how it was done, and let them haul it back in again. They only caught some seaweed, some driftwood and a jellyfish, but this didn't dampen the boys' new-found enthusiasm for fishing. They were disappointed when Dave and Bill turned the boat back to land.

"Do we have to get back?"

"You do. Your teachers will be looking for you by now. They'll be worried about what's happened to you."

Kipper and Andrew realised that this was true. And Mr Foster wasn't going to be happy when he found out what they had done.

"What do you have to do to be a fisherman?" Kipper asked, trying to change the subject. He picked up the Cavemen tin again as Dave helped Andrew ashore.

Dave and Bill laughed, winked at each other and told him to come back in six years' time. Kipper had already decided to do just that. Being a fisherman looked like a brilliant life. Your own boat to muck about in, the whole sea to sail on and nobody telling you not to get wet, or – judging by the state of Dave and Bill's overalls – to keep clean.

He and Andrew waved at the boat as it chugged off into the distance, then they turned and ran up a tarmac path to the top of the cliffs, Kipper still clutching his buried treasure.

At the top of the path was an orange telephone box, on a pole, with the words EMERGENCY – COAST-GUARD written on it. Kipper barely gave it a glance as he ran by. He was no longer bothered about not having been rescued by the coastguard. Nothing could have topped that trip in the fishing boat.

"We've been gone hours," panted Andrew as they ran. "Bet they're all out looking for us. Hey! Did you hear something?"

They stopped. The sound came faintly again, from the foot of the cliffs.

"*Hello! Hello – Help!*"

Kipper and Andrew stared at each other. There was something familiar about that voice.

Peering over the edge of the cliffs, they could just see a figure on what remained of the rocky promontory.

"Fossil-face!" gasped Andrew.

Kipper waved " *Sir!*" he yelled. " *Hello, sir!*"

The figure looked up. It bellowed something else which might have been " *Mackenzie!*" but the boys couldn't be

sure. Kipper cupped his hand to his mouth and yelled at the top of his healthy young voice.

"DON'T GET OFF ROCKS! STRONG CURRENT!"

The distant sound of an irate Maths teacher exploding floated to their ears.

"He probably can't hear you," said Andrew. "And anyway, he can't stay on those rocks much longer. Dave and Bill said they get covered at high water . . ."

The boys stared at each other. Then Kipper yelled "Come on!" and ran back towards the orange phone box.

Ten minutes later, with bated breath, they witnessed the enthralling sight of an air-sea rescue helicopter hovering over the rocks.

As he saw Mr Foster, swinging in a harness in mid-air, being winched slowly up towards the hovering helicopter, Kipper let out a deep sigh. He'd gone off fishing boats. Mentally, he revised his future career. He was going to be a coastguard helicopter pilot.

"Don't some people have all the luck?" he said enviously.

They watched for a few more moments, in silence. Then Andrew said slowly, "That could've been *us* down there ... and there might not've been anyone to call the coast-guard."

They considered this, and shuddered suddenly. It had at last dawned on them that this time they'd gone over the limit. And they'd been lucky.

"He was down there looking for us," said Andrew. "We're going to be in dead lumber."

Kipper nodded. "Well ... maybe he'll be grateful to us for saving his life," he suggested optimistically.

Which just proved, Kipper reflected an hour later, as they stood in the teachers' common room, how wrong it was possible to be.

Mr Foster was in a megolithic temper. He had been soaked, frozen and scared; he had lost a perfectly good pair of shoes in the sea, and the coastguard had given him a ticking-off about being on those rocks. And the know-ledge that the boys had witnessed his ignominious rescue did not make all this any easier to bear.

"You're a pair of silly, irresponsible little lunatics! Wandering off like that – going back to that dangerous cave – risking your blasted necks, *and* mine ..."

"But, sir," Kipper protested, "we had a good reason, sir, and we found this ..."

He held out the Cavemen tin. Mr Foster snatched it and banged it down on a table. It was Mrs Tandy who picked it up and examined it.

"Be *quiet*, you stupid little boy! Have you any idea of the blasted silly stunt you pulled? Do you *realise* what could have *happened* to you?"

The boys nodded.

"Go to your room," Mr Foster said between his teeth, "and stay there until supper. When we get back to school, in a week's time, you two are going *straight* to the Headmaster. If I had my way, I'd send you home right away. Now *go*!"

Kipper and Andrew left the room, but Kipper hesitated in the doorway.

"Can we have our tin back, please, sir?"

"NO!" roared Mr Foster. "Now GET OUT!"

He collapsed into a chair with a shudder as they left.

"You know, Bob," said Mrs Tandy, idly turning the pages of the exercise-book, "at least they did the right thing in calling the coastguard to you."

"Then it's the only right thing they did . . . Blast it, Rita, this is only the first afternoon. We haven't been here one night yet, and Mackenzie and his mob have struck already!"

"Hmm?" Mrs Tandy wasn't listening. "Good heavens – look at this. A *Beano* from 1954."

Mr Foster sat up. A sudden look of interest had entered his eyes.

"1954?" he said.

54

Half an hour later, Kipper, Andrew and the twins passed the teachers' common room on their way down to supper. The door was half-open, and they could clearly see Mr Foster, lolling in a chair, contentedly smoking his pipe. They stopped dead in their tracks.

"He's reading our comic!" gasped Andrew.

They stared at each other. Then Maya whispered, "I suppose . . . in 1954 . . . he'd have been – probably sort of about our age."

"What, *him*?" said Andrew incredulously. "Wearing short trousers like the Cavemen?"

"And *reading comics*?" echoed Rasheeda.

Kipper shook his head. "No way," he said. "Not old Fossil-face!"

As they crept past, Mr Foster smiled to himself, and turned the page to the next adventure of Lord Snooty . . .

5

Murder Most Foul

THE next morning after breakfast, as the first-formers were preparing for the day's outing to historic Sudbury Castle, Mrs Tandy quietly returned the Cavemen tin and its contents to Kipper.

"Just keep it out of Mr Foster's sight," she advised. "And this does *not* mean I condone what you did. It was very dangerous. I want you to promise me, *no* more scrambling about on the cliffs without permission. Is that clear?"

Kipper nodded. "Yes, Miss . . . Mrs Tandy, I've been thinking. I know the cliffs are out of bounds, but . . ."

"But *nothing*, Christopher," said Mrs Tandy sternly.

"No, listen," Kipper urged. "Could we go back just once more at the end of the week – if you and Mr Foster came with us?"

Mrs Tandy looked at him. He seemed serious enough. "Why? To put the tin back?"

"Sort of . . . see, like I said, we've been thinking. It's sort of like a time capsule, isn't it, Miss – buried in 1954?"

Mrs Tandy nodded thoughtfully, and agreed that it had certainly worked out that way, whether the original boys had intended it or not.

"Well, then, why don't *we* do one? A time capsule of us on this holiday. We could collect photos and souvenirs and stuff everywhere we go this week, couldn't we – and bury it back in that cave before we go?"

Mrs Tandy considered the idea. She rather liked it. And the four young faces before her were alight with enthusiasm.

"Can we, Miss?" pleaded Rasheeda. "Do our own time capsule?"

"Well," said Mrs Tandy slowly, "I don't see why not . . . but what would you use for your capsule?"

"Isn't there a biscuit tin in the catering stuff, Miss?" asked Maya, shyly. "That's what the Cavemen used."

Mrs Tandy remembered that there was. "It won't be empty until the end of the week, of course, when we've finished the biscuits, but you can have it then, I'm sure. And, meanwhile, you can start getting together things you'd like to put in your capsule. Wait there!"

She fetched her camera and took a photo of the four of them, outside the hostel; and then she talked the coach driver into taking another of the whole group, including the members of staff, just before they set off on the outing.

"Those were the last two photos on this reel of film," she explained, "so I can drop it off at the local chemist's, and they'll be developed before the end of the week, in time to go in your capsule."

As he boarded the coach, Kipper reflected that there ought by law to be a few more teachers like Mrs Tandy around.

The castle itself was half an hour by coach from the hostel. It was a huge, grey building, surrounded by fields, and by the coach park was a small area of woodland and a large lake.

Mr Foster organised the first-formers into pairs, gave them a lecture on not straying, not touching anything, not talking above whispers and several other "nots" to which Kipper paid little or no attention. Then they marched up to the castle entrance, where a middle-aged woman in navy-blue uniform was waiting to show them around. She was thin, with yellow hair, and had a pinched, sharp face and a pinched, sharp voice to match it.

Kipper, Andrew and Rasheeda endured the trek round the castle with dogged patience. The splendours of the six-teenth-century dining hall left them unmoved. The Long Gallery with its portraits of stiff and starchy-looking men and women in stiff and starchy-looking costumes barely rated a glance from them. The fine collection of eighteenth-century porcelain figurines set them yawning. All the while the guide's pinched, sharp voice went on and on explaining the history of the castle and the value of its art treasures.

"Any questions so far?" she asked eventually.

"Why's that bit fenced off?" Kipper wanted to know, pointing to a thick, red rope that stretched across the bot-

tom of a marble staircase. A sign saying PRIVATE –
NO ENTRY hung from it.

The guide explained coldly that it led to the East Wing
where the present Lord Sudbury lived.

"His apartments are closed to members of the public.
As are his private gardens. Now! Follow me and we shall
visit the dungeons."

Kipper's spirits rose at once. This was more like it. He
was first in line following the guide down the narrow,
dark, winding stone steps to the dank, damp dungeons
below.

The guide flashed a torch around. "The dungeons were
originally part of the old castle," she began, "built in 1170
on the site of the present . . ."

"I bet there's bodies down here," said Kipper.

Maya shuddered.

"No, I mean *old* ones. People who've been murdered
or starved to death hundreds of years ago . . . There's always
murders done in old places like this. I've read about 'em.
I read this one once where this Earl murdered this girl
because she wouldn't marry him, so he had her done in
and buried her in the dungeons. But her ghost came back
and haunted him, and he went mad and drowned himself
in the moat and –"

A sharp prod in the back from Mr Foster silenced him.
The Co., and several other first-formers who had been
listening avidly, reluctantly turned their attention back to
the guide's far less interesting narrative. She fixed Kipper
with a glare and went on explaining that the dungeons
had not been in use since the thirteenth century.

"That's *her* story," muttered Kipper. "I bet there's
bodies buried under us right now. I tell you there's *always*
murders in these old places."

They left the dungeons with regret, and followed the
guide upstairs to the armoury. This housed a splendid collection of fearsome-looking spears, pikes, axes, swords, daggers

and crossbows. Suits of armour, dark with age, stood everywhere. Kipper's fascinated gaze scanned the room.

"Cor, look at that sword. Bet you could have someone's head off in one swipe with that."

"Yeah! And then you could chop the body up with one of those axes, before you buried it in the – "

Both Kipper and Andrew felt a sharp prod this time. They lapsed into whispers.

The tour did not spend nearly enough time in the armoury for the boys' liking. Before long, they were out in the castle shop, looking through the souvenirs on sale. There were T-shirts, guide books, pencil-sharpeners shaped like the castle, erasers, pens and pencils, fruit-scented soaps and bath salts, tins of fudge and humbugs, badges and carstickers, all with pictures of the castle on them. Kipper liked the look of a model knight in armour, but put it down hastily when he saw the price – over five pounds. In the end, they clubbed together and bought their first souvenir for their time capsule – a Sudbury Castle ballpoint-pen and small notebook.

This was not exactly what they had wanted for their capsule, but it would come in useful; Maya could write the accompanying notes in the notebook with the pen. As the best writer and speller of the group, she had unanimously been elected to this task.

Out in the grounds of the castle, the first-formers ate packed lunches of ham sandwiches, apples, chocolate biscuits and crisps. Then Miss Lambe handed out questionnaires.

"Now, then," she said brightly, "these are for you to do the wildlife trail. You have one hour before we get the coach home. You follow the trail through the woods down to the lake, and you tick off all the species of ducks and geese that are listed on these sheets. You see you've got little pictures of all of them to help you find them. Won't that be fun? It'll be just like a little treasure hunt. Don't wander from the path, and you can't possibly get lost. We'll be sitting here if you want us. Off you go, then."

Kipper and Co. followed their form mates. Their minds were not, however, on pictures of ducks and geese.

"Let's play Ghosthunters," suggested Kipper. "You three are ghosts of people who've been horribly murdered here, and I'm out to find you and blast you to bits with my anti-ectoplasm disintegrator-gun. I'll give you fifty. GO!"

The ghosts scattered, emitting gruesome howls and moans, while their hunter ducked behind a tree, counted rapidly to fifty, then sprang out and set off at a run to begin searching for his victims.

It was pretty obvious, he figured, that they wouldn't have headed for the lake; it was too open, and there was nowhere to hide around it. So he kept around the trees and bushes, but the ghosts had dematerialised very successfully. There was no sign of them.

A high privet hedge ran down one edge of the trees. Kipper went over to it, and grinned to himself. There was a small hole at the bottom of it – a small, just-about-eleven-year-old-person-sized hole . . .

He got down on all fours and squeezed through the gap in the hedge, scratching himself and tearing his T-shirt in the process.

On the other side was a wide expanse of green rolling hillside dotted around with oak-trees. The field led up to some neatly laid-out gardens and a fountain, and from there to a wing of the castle. Kipper remembered the guide saying something about a private part of the house where Lord Sudbury lived. This must be it.

Oh, well, it was miles to the castle from here, and if anyone *was* looking out of a private window, they'd never see him, not all this distance away. He was about to turn away and resume his search for his ghostly companions when suddenly he froze.

Two figures – a young man, and a girl – were strolling out from the formal garden.

Kipper looked around frantically, then darted to the nearest oak-tree and scrambled up it. Its thick, gnarled trunk provided several good hand and footholds, and in seconds Kipper was hidden among the branches.

He watched with bated breath as the young man and girl approached. From the casual way they were chatting, Kipper guessed that they had not noticed the juvenile trespasser in their oak-tree.

Soon their voices floated to his ears.

"We're better out of the house right now," the youth was saying. "What with the fuss Aunt Edwina's causing. She's turning the place upside down, and she's got all the staff on to it, too."

"Oh, poor Lady Sudbury," said the young woman

sympathetically. "She *is* fond of that brooch."

To Kipper's dismay, they paused right under the tree. The youth leaned back against it.

"Oh, don't feel too sorry for her," he said. "It was the same when she mislaid her pearl necklace last week. She had everyone going crazy searching for it, and it turned up two days later in her room, not lost at all."

Kipper almost yawned. He wished they'd shove off so that he could get down and go on looking for his ghosts. One thing that being up this tree had convinced him of was that they hadn't come through the hedge to hide after all. He could see for miles around, and they weren't anywhere . . .

Suddenly his attention jerked back to the youth, who had taken a notebook out of his pocket.

"Now. While we've got some peace, let's work out the details . . . How am I going to get rid of Lord Sudbury?"

Kipper's eyes flew wide open. WHAT had he said?

"Oh, poison might be the best thing," said the girl casually. "It would certainly be the easiest to do. You could slip some poison into his wine."

The young man nodded. "I *could* . . . but it might be better to stab him. There are some daggers in the armoury that would do the job nicely. I could use one of those."

Kipper's jaw had dropped. He couldn't be hearing this. Not for real.

"You could wear a mask," the girl suggested, "and creep up on him when he's asleep . . ."

"Excellent!" said the young man, making notes on his pad. "I must hide my identity. Obviously no one must suspect that I've killed my uncle, or I wouldn't inherit his title, would I? We'll have to cover my tracks carefully. I suppose there wouldn't be a problem with the blood?"

"Oh, you leave that to me," said the girl with a smile. "I can cope with a little blood."

They wandered on, out of earshot.

Kipper waited for a few moments, then slid down out

of the tree, unsteadily. His mind was racing. He'd seen plays and films where uncles and nephews murdered each other to inherit titles – people were always doing that in history, he knew. But somehow, this was different. This was real. And he was the only person who knew what was going to happen.

He shuddered, and shook himself. There was only one thing to do. Find Lord Sudbury and warn him against his plotting nephew – and fast.

He checked quickly to make sure the coast was clear, and then he darted full speed towards the castle, taking short cuts across neat lawns, dodging around the fountain with its four corner statues of lions, leaping across ornamental flowerbeds until he reached the huge, oak front door. He hammered on it loudly.

He heard footsteps from inside, then the thick wooden door creaked open. A fat, balding man with white sideburns stood glaring pompously down at him.

"I've got to see Lord Sudbury," panted Kipper. "Are you him?"

The fat man's face reddened. He drew himself up. "I am his lordship's butler," he snapped, "and *you* are trespassing."

Kipper drew a deep breath.

"They're going to stab him with a dagger from the armoury. I heard them. It's his nephew . . ."

The fat butler's face had now reached a shade of deep puce. He grabbed Kipper by the top of his arm.

"This is private property. Members of the public are *not* allowed in here." He began to drag the struggling and protesting Kipper towards a gate. "I shall find out which school you are with, and launch a strong complaint . . ."

Kipper gave up trying to explain. If he wanted to save Lord Sudbury, it was time for action.

He kicked the butler's fat ankle, hard; and while the butler yelled and hopped around clutching his foot, Kipper wrenched free and raced back towards the castle at top speed.

The butler came pounding after him. The pomposity had left his manner, and he was bellowing in a fashion that would have done credit to old Fossil-face.

"You little . . . You wait till I get you!"

Kipper was not waiting. He nipped smartly into the castle through the front door which the butler had left open, and slammed it shut in the butler's face, to slow him up. Then he set off through the castle corridors, opening each door as he passed it and looking into each room. He *had* to find Lord Sudbury.

In one large, sunny room was an elderly white-haired lady who was moving the cushions around on an elegant sofa, picking them up and peering under them, then replacing them and patting them back into their previous smooth shapes. As Kipper opened the door, she looked up, a vague expression on her pleasant, mild face. She lifted a pair of spectacles that were hanging on a thin gold chain around her neck, and peered at him through them.

"Oh, hello," she said. "I don't suppose you've found it, by any chance?"

Kipper was taken aback. "What?" he asked, blinking.

"My brooch," said the old lady, mildly. "I thought per-

haps they'd sent you to help in the search. You *are* the cook's son, aren't you? I did tell them to get everyone to look."

"Lord Sudbury," said Kipper urgently, unwilling to be sidetracked. "Where is he?"

The old lady looked surprised. "In the gardens, I believe, dear, but I don't quite see what that has to do with –"

She was interrupted by a shout. Kipper turned around, saw the fat butler descending on him, and fled.

"Strange boy," murmured the old lady into thin air.

Kipper ran on, his mind spinning. So Lord Sudbury was out in the gardens – which was just where the conspirators were! What if they'd gone and got the dagger from the armoury already? They might decide to get him, then and there, and not bother about waiting till he was asleep.

Kipper took a wide marble flight of stairs in leaps, three steps at a time, swung himself around the balcony at the top and sped off along another corridor. The fat butler was still panting along behind him, but he was falling further behind with each step. Kipper saw his chance to hide, throw the butler off his trail, and then go out into the gardens again to find Lord Sudbury before the murderers did. He galloped up another smaller flight of stairs and along another corridor. There were three doors ahead of him, and he yanked open the first and dived through it.

He was standing in a small bedroom containing a single bed, a small chest of drawers and a wardrobe. Kipper paused, then suddenly heard the butler's heavy footsteps pounding up the stairs. He opened the wardrobe door, wriggled in amongst the clothing and crouched down on some shoes, pulling the door shut after him, but leaving it open just a fraction of a centimetre, to make sure he didn't get locked in.

The bedroom door crashed open. Kipper could hear the

butler gasping and wheezing hoarsely for breath. He held
his own breath, crossed all his fingers and closed his eyes,
hoping against hope that the butler had not seen him go
into the room.

And then the door slammed again, and the butler was
gone.

Kipper let his breath out slowly. He'd thought he'd had
it that time.

He waited, counted to fifty slowly to give the coast time
to clear, and then pushed open the wardrobe very, very
quietly, and crept out.

The door handle turned again. Kipper spun round and
darted back into the wardrobe.

He had just pulled the wardrobe door to behind him
again when someone entered the room. It couldn't be the
fat butler – "it" wasn't panting and wheezing nearly
enough. Kipper peered through the crack of the wardrobe
door.

It was the sharp-voiced, yellow-haired castle guide.

6

Jewel Thieves

KIPPER almost groaned aloud. Just his luck! What did *she* have to come in here for right now? He had a feeling that she'd be sure to recognise him if he left the wardrobe. And what's more, he didn't think that she'd believe him for one minute if he tried to convince her that there was a plot against Lord Sudbury's life. She didn't seem the sort of person who would believe anything a mere boy told her. She'd probably just hand him straight over to that butler.

He thought quickly. There must be *some* way he could explain things to her to make her understand how serious it was. He *had* to try, because it was obvious she wasn't leaving the room again in a hurry. She had just sat down on the bed.

He was still trying to work out exactly how to put it, when the door opened yet again and a girl of about nineteen, in a green overall and a white apron, entered. She had the same yellow hair and pinched nose as the guide.

Watching through the crack of the wardrobe door, Kipper saw the guide cross swiftly to the door of the bedroom, look up and down the corridor, then close the door again very quietly.

"Got anything yet?" she asked, turning to the girl.

The girl held out a fist and dropped something into the guide's outstretched palm. Kipper stifled a gasp. He had caught sight of a small, round, shiny object.

The guide frowned. "Is this *all*? Come on, Alice, you've got the run of the old girl's entire boudoir."

The girl's voice sounded sulky. "It's not *my* fault if she's taken to locking her jewellery drawer, is it? She got jumpy after that necklace was gone for two days last week. She left this brooch pinned to the dress she was wearing yesterday; that's how I got it. And you'd better hurry and get the copy made. She's got everyone looking for it as it is."

She broke off abruptly as the door burst open. The guide hastily slipped her hand into her pocket. The fat butler stood there, purple-cheeked and heaving.

"Mr Parsons!" said the guide icily. "What is the meaning of this? How dare you burst into my daughter's room?"

But Mr Parsons ignored her. He had seen the wardrobe door twitch very slightly.

"Ah-HA!" he roared, stepping forward and wrenching the door open.

A small missile shot out of the wardrobe, ramming him hard amidships and knocking all the remaining breath from his body. He hit the carpet with a bump and sprawled there, spluttering.

The guide and the girl both screamed.

Kipper was out of the room and gone.

As he bounded down the stairs, he tried to sort out what he'd overheard. Things were getting worse and worse. Not only was Lord Sudbury's nephew a would-be assassin, but the yellow-haired guide was a thief! She and her daughter were obviously posing as castle employees in order to steal old Lady Sudbury's jewels. He ought to warn the old lady ... No. There was a more urgent matter still at hand. Lord Sudbury wasn't safe. Kipper had to get out into the gardens and warn him first; then, when his life was no longer in danger, he could tell him about the thieves. The police could round them all up together, the thieves and the would-be murderers.

Crikey! And today had started as just a dull old outing to a boring old castle!

He fled down the marble staircase, dragged open the thick wooden front door and escaped into the gardens.

As he ran towards the fountain, there was a bellow from the castle. Parsons the butler was leaning out of an upstairs window, pointing at him and shouting.

"Stop that boy! STOP THAT BOY!"

A gardener, shears in hand, appeared from behind one of the ornamental hedges. He saw Kipper, gave a shout of "Hoi! You!", dropped the shears and gave chase.

Kipper didn't hang around. The gardener looked none too friendly. He took off with the gardener right behind him.

Unlike Parsons, who was middle-aged and very fat, the gardener was young and fit, and Kipper had to put all his effort into keeping in front of him. They dodged around the fountain, zig-zagged across the lawns and out into the field, the gardener gaining on Kipper all the time.

Weaving to try and throw off his pursuer, Kipper ducked around one of the oak-trees and collided heavily with the would-be murderer.

The girl gave a squeal of surprise as Lord Sudbury's nephew crashed to the ground. The gardener, who had just charged round the tree hot on Kipper's tail, tripped and fell too. Kipper gave a yell of triumph.

"Hold him!" he yelled. "He's the murderer!" and he flung himself on top of both of them.

The girl promptly grabbed him and pulled him off. Her face was flushed with anger. She was surprisingly strong for a slim girl. "What *do* you think you're doing!" she cried.

The gardener and the youth rose groggily to their feet. Kipper tried to pull free of the girl. He could see Parsons the butler puffing towards them.

"They're here!" he shouted. "This is them –"

His words were choked off as Parson got him once again by the scruff of his neck and started to shake him. Kipper wrestled to pull free.

"Him – and her!" he panted. "I heard them! They're going to stab him and poison him, and . . ."

The youth, who had been dusting himself down, stopped and stared at Kipper. "What?" he demanded. "Parsons, let him go."

Reluctantly, Parsons obliged. Kipper backed away a few steps, ready to run if he wasn't believed and the murderers turned nasty.

"I heard you," he said nervously. "You're going to stab him, and *she's* going to cope with the blood, and it's so *you* can be Lord Sudbury!"

"Are you *mad*?" bellowed Parsons.

"But I *am* Lord Sudbury," said the youth.

Kipper's voice choked in his throat. "W-what?" he gasped.

"He *is* Lord Sudbury," said Parsons, with satisfaction. "And *you*, boy, are in *trouble*."

Kipper was staring from Lord Sudbury to the girl and back again. "But ..." he protested feebly. "But ... you said ..."

Suddenly, to his amazement, he saw that Lord Sudbury's shoulders were shaking with mirth.

The girl was laughing too, so much that she could hardly speak.

"I was talking about blood capsules!" she gasped out at last. "We're putting on a pageant next Bank Holiday here at the castle. We're doing the story of the evil third Lord Sudbury, who was supposed to have murdered his uncle for the title – in 1547!"

Kipper began to turn a dull red. "Oh," he said, shuffling his feet.

"And I'm playing him," explained Lord Sudbury, between hoots of merriment. "Oh dear, oh dear ... you've been rushing round trying to save me from murdering myself!"

Kipper's blush had now spread right up to the roots of his gingery-red hair. Trust him to get the wrong end of the stick. For once, he was glad that Andrew and the twins weren't there to see him make a right wally of himself.

Even the knowledge that he'd been right about there being a good murder story linked with the castle's history couldn't comfort him. He felt utterly stupid.

"Oh," he mumbled again. "I didn't know, honest. And

I s'pose they just needed that jewellery to make copies for costumes."

Suddenly Lord Sudbury and the girl stopped laughing. They were staring at him. So was Parsons.

"What?" they all said together. "Who did?"

Kipper could have kicked himself. Why hadn't he shut up? Now he'd have to explain about that other embarrassing mistake he'd made.

So, hesitantly, he told them about the yellow-haired guide, the girl Alice, and the brooch and the necklace. And then, to his surprise, Lord Sudbury took him by the arm and hurried him back to the castle. Parsons and the girl followed, leaving the gardener scratching his head and reflecting that he'd worked for the nobility for years, and they got barmier all the time.

The old lady was in the hall when they arrived, searching behind a vase of flowers. Lord Sudbury took her gently by the arm. "Aunt Edwina," he said, "I'd like you to come to your jewellery drawer and take a close look at your pearl necklace – the one you lost last week and then found again."

The old lady looked slightly puzzled as they escorted her upstairs. But as she entered her boudoir, she gave a little cry of delight.

"Oh, my brooch! Now however did it get there? It wasn't there earlier!"

The brooch was lying on top of her dressing-table. The

old lady picked it up.

"They put it back because they knew I'd seen 'em with it!" cried Kipper excitedly.

"Exactly," said Lord Sudbury. "Getting rid of the evidence. But that won't save them. We've still got the pearl necklace. Aunty?"

The old lady unlocked her jewellery drawer, and Lord Sudbury lifted out a pearl necklace. "Hmm," he said, turning it over in his hand. "Did *your* pearl necklace have such a shiny new clasp?"

"No, it didn't," said the old lady, peering at the necklace. "Good gracious! Do you mean this isn't mine?"

"I mean it isn't even pearl," said Lord Sudbury.

"They've had it made specially so they could put it in place of yours, and you wouldn't notice yours had been nicked!" said Kipper.

"And when we've proved this to be a fake, we've got 'em," agreed Lord Sudbury with satisfaction. "Parsons, ring the police. They'll have done a bunk, but they won't have got far."

Parsons, who had been staring open-mouthed, swallowed hard, closed his mouth and left the room.

"Sly pair," observed Lord Sudbury. "Stealing the jewellery piece by piece, and replacing 'em with fakes in the hope no one would notice. Could have been a long time before anyone did, too, if you hadn't heard them plotting. You'd better stay here till the police come. They'll want a statement from you. You're an important witness!"

Kipper swelled with pride. He'd helped to prevent a crime after all – even if it wasn't the one he'd thought he was preventing. Wait till he told the others . . .

Then suddenly he remembered. Miss Lambe had said the coach would be leaving in an hour. And that was – crikey! He checked his watch. Fifty-five minutes ago! Old Fossil-face would blow a fuse if he was late back.

He explained to Lord Sudbury, but his lordship smiled

74

and said he would explain things to his teacher, and then run Kipper back to the hostel later on, when the police had spoken with him. Kipper's eyes shone.

"Yeah, great!" he enthused.

At the coach park, Mr Foster, Mrs Tandy and Miss Lambe were just rounding up all the pupils. Mr Foster wasn't at all surprised that one of them was still missing, even though the hour was up.

"Mackenzie. Wouldn't you know if we had to hold the coach up for someone, it would be that boy. Andrew Quine, where is he?"

Andrew and the twins were at a loss to answer. They hadn't seen Kipper since the beginning of the ghost game. After ten minutes, they'd got bored of hiding and gone looking for him, but he hadn't turned up, and they couldn't think what had happened to him.

Then Quentin Parslow, smirking, pointed and said, "He's just coming now, sir. He's been back in the castle, sir, when you told us not to. And there's someone with him, sir."

His triumphant smirk widened as Kipper joined them.

" *You're* for it," he hissed.

Kipper grinned. "Sorry, mate. Not this time."

He turned his back on the gaping Parslow, and as Lord Sudbury began talking to an astonished Mr Foster, Kipper explained things, very quickly, to the Co. as they clustered around him.

The police, when they arrived, were a little disappointing. They didn't roar up to the castle in a posse of panda cars and screech to a halt with sirens blaring and lights flashing, as Kipper had hoped. Instead, a young constable arrived quietly and insisted on taking statements from everyone, beginning with Lady Edwina and Lord Sudbury and his fiancée, before he got round to Kipper.

None the less, Kipper's was the star testament, and he enjoyed telling it. And he enjoyed even more the trip to the castle shop with Lord Sudbury, and – most of all – the high-speed journey back to the hostel in a gleaming Porsche.

That evening he was the centre of attention, and over supper in the dining-room, while Andrew and the twins admired the model knights in armour which Lord Sudbury had bought for them at Kipper's request, Kipper told his story over and over again, with a few embellishments which had since come to him.

"He gave us that stuff as a thank-you for helping to catch the thieves. The cop said they'd nabbed 'em before they'd got five miles away. They're part of a notorious gang of jewel thieves. They were planning to steal all the jewels and all the valuable works of art in the castle, bit by bit, till I overheard 'em plotting. The police reckon they're just spokes in a vast international wheel of crime. Probably it saved all the other castles and big houses in England now that the police are on to this gang, and . . ."

Mrs Tandy had picked up the guide-book that lay beside him on the table. "Where did this come from?" she asked.

"Him," said Kipper. "That's for our time capsule. I told him all about it."

Mrs Tandy opened the book at the flyleaf and read the inscription written there. It read "*To Kipper and the new Cavemen, from the murderous Edwin, Lord Sudbury*".

"Whatever does that mean?" she asked.

Kipper smiled innocently.

"Oh, probably just something he felt like writing in it, Miss," he said.

7

Willis Mark II

EVERYONE had heard of the Cavemen tin by now, but Kipper and Co. guarded it well. It was theirs, and once they'd allowed the others to view the contents, they stashed it away carefully, taking it in turns to read the comic but leaving the rest untouched. The penknife might have proved a greater temptation if it had not been broken as well as very rusty, but, as Kipper said, if it *had* been usable one of the adults would probably have taken it off them anyway. Fossil-face was famous for confiscating penknives; he'd had two off Kipper and one off Andrew already that term.

The Cavemen tin accompanied Kipper and Co. when next morning the group set off for the nearby local campsite and the nights under canvas which the holiday had promised.

The site was a large field a few miles away, with houses at one edge of it and trees at the other. In the centre of the field were about twenty small green tents, set in a circle around a large white tent. Mr Foster gathered the first-formers together and told them to pair up and select a tent.

"Girls on that side of the field, boys on this. No one is to go into the big tent without permission; that's the catering tent. And you are to keep away from the houses at all times. Got that?"

There was a murmur which could have been "Yes, sir."

"I said, have we got that!"

"Yes, SIR!"

"Right! Split up and choose your tents. Mackenzie, Quine – I'll have you two in this one. Next to mine!"

Kipper and Andrew looked at each other and grimaced. They'd been planning to see which tent Fossil-face chose, and then pick one as far away from it as possible.

They dumped their knapsacks and their Cavemen tin in the tent indicated, and then set off to explore the campsite. But Mr Foster called them back. The day had been well planned and organised. Twenty-four of the group were to go on a three-mile ramble with Mr Foster and Miss Lambe, while the other eight stayed behind with Mrs Tandy to help her prepare lunch. To Kipper's annoyance, he and Rasheeda were in the eight to stay behind, and Andrew and Maya weren't.

Worse still, Quentin Parslow was staying too. Fancy clumping him into a group with old Parsnip-features.

He scowled darkly as Andrew, Maya and the others trudged away. It wasn't that he minded the cooking – in fact, he fancied being put in charge of one of the two barbecues on which sausages were beginning to sizzle. But Mrs Tandy handed him and Rasheeda two big, empty water-containers, and pointed at a long, low, stone building at one end of the field.

"Those are the washrooms. You'll find the tap for drinking water outside. You'll need to do two or three trips, I should think."

Sighing heavily, Kipper and Rasheeda set off. Quentin Parslow was already smirking behind one of the two barbecues, tongs in hand.

"Teacher's pet," muttered Rasheeda.

They found the tap and filled the containers, then set off back towards the tents, pretending to be weighed down by the water. They staggered this way and that, their free arms waving wildly.

Suddenly Rasheeda stopped, looking puzzled. "Who are *they*?" she said.

Three boys were advancing across the field towards them from the direction of the houses. They were not part of the Rexley Manor group; that was obvious even from a distance. As they drew nearer, Kipper could see that one of them, a boy of about fourteen, had a strangely familiar, spotty, pugnacious face.

"Hoi!" this youth addressed them. "You lot from Leatherham? Rexley Manor school, right?"

Kipper and Rasheeda stopped in surprise. The three youths positioned themselves in front of them, blocking their way.

"I said, you from Rexley Manor?"

"What if we are?" enquired Kipper.

The pugnacious one leered. "My cousin goes to your school," he informed them. "My cousin Darren. Darren *Willis*."

Realisation dawned on Kipper. No wonder the boy had seemed familiar. He had more than a look of Willis of 2X about him. Just their luck, to come hundreds of miles from home and find a Willis clone.

"And he told me you'd be here sometime this week," continued Willis's cousin. "We want one of you. A kid called Mackenzie."

Kipper put down the water-container.

"He said he was a grotty little ginger-nob," continued Willis Mark II. "It better not be *you*, kid."

Kipper squared up to him. "What are you going to do about it?" he demanded.

The three boys closed in on him at once. Willis's cousin jabbed him in the shoulder, painfully, with a stubby finger.

"My cousin Darren don't like you, kid. And that means I don't like you neither. We don't want you in our field. Got that?"

"It isn't *your* field," said Rasheeda boldly. "It's a council campsite, so tough."

Willis's cousin ignored her, and jabbed Kipper again. Kipper smacked his hand away and the fight was about to begin in earnest when Mrs Tandy's voice suddenly rang out.

"STOP THAT!"

The three boys fell back. Mrs Tandy was advancing on them, her eyes glinting in anger.

"What's going on here? You boys aren't from this camp!"

They glowered but didn't answer. Mrs Tandy was generally even-tempered but when she was annoyed her voice grew sharper than splinters.

"I said, *are* you? Right. Then you can leave this field. Now."

Willis's cousin and his mates began to edge away. Then with a final glare and a threatening fist-clenched gesture at Kipper, they turned and stomped off.

Quentin Parslow was lurking behind Mrs Tandy, grinning. The information which he'd just overhead had been very interesting.

"Please, Miss, it was Christopher Mackenzie who started that fight. I saw him – "

"Nobody asked you to tell tales," said Mrs Tandy crisply. "And I didn't give you permission to leave the barbecue. Get back to it at once and don't leave it unattended again. And *none* of you is to have anything more to do with any of those boys from the village. Is that clear?"

Kipper nodded, but he had a sneaking suspicion that he had not seen the last of Willis's cousin.

Before long, the other twenty-four pupils were back and sniffing hungrily at the appetising smell of barbecued sausages. While they ate their hot-dogs, Kipper told Andrew and Maya about Willis's cousin. Andrew frowned.

"If they come back, we'll be ready for 'em."

"Too right." Kipper rather hoped they did. With Andrew at his side, he'd gladly take on the three of them. Could be a good fight.

After lunch, they were all left to their own devices for half an hour, with a strict warning from Mr Foster not to leave the field. Kipper and Andrew joined in an impromptu game of football with some of the other boys, and the twins found some space and began to practise handstands. The Co. were all so busy and absorbed in what they were doing that none of them noticed Quentin

81

Parslow and Nigel Bailey quietly creeping off to the edge of the field, by the houses, where three figures were hanging about.

Willis's cousin scowled as he saw them approaching. Quentin Parslow hastily held up two crossed fingers.

"Fainites," he said quickly.

"What d' *you* want?" snapped Willis's cousin.

"It's all right," Quentin Parslow assured him, "we're on *your* side. We just wanted to tell you how you can get at Mackenzie, if you want to."

"Yeah?" Willis's cousin eyed them suspiciously. "Why'd you want to do that, then?"

"'Cause we can't stand him," said Nigel Bailey.

"Yes," agreed Quentin Parslow. "We're on your cousin's side at school, and we'll prove it. Now look. This afternoon we're all going to a nature reserve, so the camp'll be empty then. Now. See that tent there? Second from the end? That's Mackenzie's. And in it, he's got this mouldy old tin . . ."

He told Willis's cousin everything about the Cavemen. Willis Mark II's eyes glittered meanly.

Ten minutes later, Mr Foster blew three blasts on his whistle to gather everyone together. Rasheeda, her head spinning from a successful attempt at turning eight cartwheels in a row, noticed Quentin Parslow and Nigel Bailey scuttling back from the edge of the field, but she didn't think anything of it.

The outing to the nature reserve proved to be about as dull as Kipper had anticipated it would be. Miss Lambe trilled on about all the various species of birds and insects all around them, but the only moment of interest came when she provided them with bread to bomb the ducks. However, the ammunition ran out too soon, and the afternoon resumed its slow, boring pace. Kipper began to look forward keenly to resuming their interrupted game of football back at the camp before the big potato-bake that night.

He noticed Quentin Parslow and Nigel Bailey sniggering together a few times, but didn't give it much thought until, back at the campsite, he and Andrew went into their tent at Mrs Tandy's command to change out of their wet socks and trainers, which had somehow got mud-spattered during the duck-bombing on the shores of the pond.

Kipper, the first into the tent, froze.

The Cavemen tin was not where he had left it, under his sleeping bag. It had gone.

"Nicked!" gasped Andrew.

Kipper's face darkened as he recalled those sniggers.

"Old Parsnip-features is to do with this. Let's get him and force a confession out of him!"

But Quentin Parslow and Nigel Bailey, suspecting that the reckoning might be coming, had latched on to Miss Lambe as soon as they saw Kipper and Andrew go into their tent, and were sticking close to her side, asking questions about the birds and insects they had seen that afternoon. It was impossible to tackle them, much less scrag them, with Miss Lambe there.

Then Andrew nudged Kipper sharply. At the edge of the field, by the houses, were three figures.

"Is that him?" he asked. "Willis's cousin?"

Kipper shot a quick look around. Miss Lambe was busy with Quentin Parslow and Nigel Bailey, Mrs Tandy had gone to the washroom, and Mr Foster, surrounded by several other pupils, was trying to build a camp fire for the great potato-bake later.

"Yeah, that's him. Come on!"

He signalled to the twins, and the four of them tore across the field. Willis's cousin and his mates were grinning. As Kipper and Co. drew near, they produced the Cavemen tin from behind their backs and held it high.

"Want your stupid old junk, then?"

"Yah!"

"Come and get it!" they chanted.

And they turned and ran. The Co. pursued them, with Andrew, who was small and wiry and the fastest runner, in the lead.

Willis and his gang rushed down a long alleyway between two houses, out into a street, and round a corner, the Co. following. Although they were not far behind them, by the time Kipper rounded the bend, Willis's cousin and his mob had vanished.

Andrew was standing panting in the road. He pointed to a nearby house. The side gate that led to its back garden was still swinging gently on its hinges.

"In there," he said.

Kipper's eyes narrowed. Now they knew which house Willis Mark II's was. They had him cornered.

"We'll go in after him, and grab our tin back," he told the twins. "You two stay here, in case he makes a run for it out of the front!"

And beckoning Andrew to follow, he tiptoed across the front lawn of the house and round to the side gate.

The back garden was empty. Nothing was to be seen but a lawn-mower standing abandoned in the centre of a half-mown lawn. And then, from behind a shed at the bottom of the garden, Kipper heard definite scuffling noises.

He put a finger to his lips, and gestured at the shed.

"Let's rush 'em and grab it!" he hissed.

They crept very quietly to the shed. Kipper paused,

counted down from three under his breath, whispered
"*Now!*" and the two boys darted round the side of the
shed, flung themselves behind it, and crashed into the thin,
middle-aged man who had been quietly emptying his lawn-
mower cuttings on to his compost heap. The three sprawled
in the compost together in a shower of grass cuttings, the
man yelling and coughing.

"HELP! What the – HELP! OUR TREVOR –
HELP!"

Suddenly Kipper and Andrew felt a hand on each of
their collars, and they were yanked roughly to their feet.

They looked up to see a tall, heavily-muscled young man
glowering at them.

"Right!" he growled, his grip on them tightening.
"What you doin' here, bargin' my dad around?"

Kipper gurgled. He couldn't do much else. He was being
slowly strangled. He waved his arms wildly, showering
grass and mouldy leaves around him.

". . . Willis!" he managed to croak at last.

"Oh, so that's who you are, are you?" Our Trevor shook
him. "Right, Willis, you're for it. Trespass and assault and
battery. Dad, go and ring the police!"

The thin man had crawled out of his compost and was
staggering towards the house, winded. Kipper tried again,

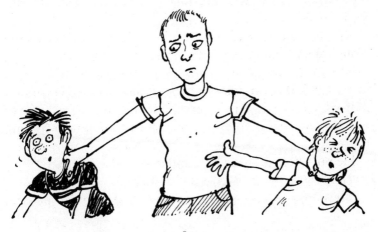

85

his face slowly turning purple as he struggled for breath.

". . . Lives here!" he spluttered. "He . . ."

His voice faded. He had suddenly realised the awful truth.

Willis's cousin did *not* live there.

He had tricked them. He had deliberately gone into the garden of the wrong house, knowing they'd see and follow. And Kipper had played right into his hands. Trespass and assault. His blood chilled at the thought of what the police would say. This was going to be a lot less pleasant than his last encounter with the constabulary.

And he didn't even want to begin thinking about what old-Fossil-face would have to say about this. Oh, crikey! Not to mention his *parents*! Because Fossil-face would be bound to tell them.

He gazed hopelessly at Andrew, who gazed hopelessly back. They were caught. Nothing for it but to wait until the police got there.

Luckily for them, that did not take long. In less than five minutes, Kipper and Andrew, released from the iron grip of Our Trevor, stood rubbing their necks and miserably trying to explain to a tall, portly policeman.

"A tin, you say?" He took out a police notebook and began to write. "And you say these boys you were pursuing had taken this tin from you."

"A likely story," snorted Trevor. "Mugging my dad, they were . . . probably after his wallet . . ."

"We *weren't*," said Kipper desperately. "We only wanted our tin, that's all."

The policeman enquired what was in the tin that had been so special, and Kipper and Andrew tried hard to remember all the contents.

"Well, there was a photo – and a comic."

"And an exercise-book – oh, and a rusty old penknife."

"We dug it up, you see . . ."

A sudden alert expression had entered the policeman's eyes. "Anything else?"

Kipper went on to explain how and where they had found the tin. The policeman had stopped writing and was listening with growing interest.

"Smugglers' Cliffs, eh?" he said.

Then, to the boys' astonishment, he put the notebook back in his pocket. His stern look had faded. He was almost smiling as he turned to Trevor and his father.

"Well, now it's been explained, sir, I'm sure you can see the boys here made a mistake. You won't be wanting to press charges, then?"

"What?" growled Trevor suspiciously. "How do we know they're telling the truth? They could've been indoors and stolen something before they came out here and mugged my dad."

At the policeman's request, Kipper and Andrew turned out their pockets. This operation produced half a grimy tissue, a stub of pencil, a dead beetle, a chewing gum wrapper, the tail end of a packet of fruit Rolos and a penny. Even Trevor had to admit, grudgingly, that none of these had come from the house.

"So I take it that's that then, sir?" enquired the policeman.

"Well, we'll let 'em off this time," muttered Trevor reluctantly. He wagged a thick finger at Kipper. "But if ever I see either of 'em round here again . . ."

He needn't worry about that, Kipper reflected, rubbing

87

the back of his neck. There was *no* way he was coming back here to be half-murdered again.

He was still dazed as the policeman ushered them both out through the side garden gate and into the street.

The twins were waiting there, looking miserable. They had seen the police car drive up and the policeman go into the house, and they knew that something must have gone horribly wrong with the boys' mission. When they saw Kipper and Andrew with the policeman, they stepped forward, swallowing hard.

"With them, are you?" said the policeman. He had assumed his stern expression again as he shook a finger at them. "Well, I'll turn a blind eye *this* time, but don't make a habit of this, all right?"

The twins' jaws dropped. They were almost certain he had just winked at them.

"Now," he said, taking out his notebook and consulting it again, "Willis, I think you said? Yes, I know the family. Live a few doors down. Come along."

Still totally fazed, the Co. followed him down the street. As if in a dream, they watched him go up to the front door of another house. Here he turned, put a finger to his lips and pointed to the side gate.

"I'll keep them busy. You slip round the back."

"But – " Kipper protested, feebly.

"Off you go!" said the policeman briskly. He rang the doorbell, and Kipper and Co. scuttled round the side of the house and peered out to watch, amazed.

"Excuse me, sir," the policeman was saying to whoever had answered the door, "but is that your car parked outside?"

A gruff voice asserted that it was.

"I couldn't help noticing that your offside rear tyre is balding, sir," said the policeman pleasantly. "Could I see your spare?"

He led an older version of Willis's cousin up the path

to the car parked outside. Quickly, Kipper saw their chance. He hustled the Co. through the side gate, and they peeked into the back garden.

There, on the lawn, with the tin between them, crouched Willis's cousin and his two mates. They were prodding the contents of the tin and sneering in contempt.

"Load of old rubbish!"

"Why'd they bother about this, anyway?"

Willis's cousin was grinning nastily. "Dead funny it was, when we led 'em into the wrong house. Wait'll my cousin Darren hears about this!"

"*Now!*" hissed Kipper, and they burst out of hiding and launched themselves at the unsuspecting threesome. Kipper grabbed Willis's cousin, who went sprawling with a yell. Andrew and Rasheeda tackled the other two and Maya snatched up all the contents and stuffed them back into the tin.

"Got it!" she panted.

"Let's GO!" yelled Kipper.

They scrambled up and rushed back around to the front of the house. Willis's cousin and his mates staggered to their feet. They had been taken by surprise and caught off-balance, but now they had regained their breath. Uttering roars of wrath, they charged after Kipper and Co.

Round the front of the house, they skidded to a halt just in time to avoid colliding with a policeman.

Willis Senior's head emerged from the boot of his car, where he had been checking on his spare tyre. He had not seen Kipper and Co. come out, but he did see his son almost knock over a policeman.

"Watch where you're going!" he snapped.

"We were chasing them kids, Dad," protested his son. "In our garden."

"Kids?" said the policeman. "I never saw any kids come out of your garden, son. Must have been looking the wrong way." He checked the spare tyre. "Well, that seems in order, sir," he said. "Change that for your offside rear, get yourself a new spare and we'll say no more about it."

He touched his helmet and strolled off round the corner, where Kipper and Co. were waiting for him, hugging the tin.

"We don't get it," said Kipper, fixing him with a straight look. "Why're you helping us?"

The policeman smiled, took the tin from Maya and opened it. He drew out the photo and pointed to the youngest and smallest boy in the front, with the shortest trousers and the grimiest knees.

"That's me," he said.

Kipper and Co. stared at him, wide-eyed.

"You're – a CAVEMAN?" gasped Kipper.

"They'd only just let me join," said the policeman. "Always said I was too young. I'm Eric's brother, Arthur." He turned the photo over. "Oh, he didn't put our names on it. Just the oath."

"Death to Traitors," said Andrew softly.

90

Arthur had opened the exercise-book, but even the first page had faded.

"Oh, well," he said with a sigh and a smile, "never mind. We never got round to writing much in it, anyway."

The Co. grinned. They knew the feeling. So far, their Sudbury Castle pen had not been put to much use either.

Arthur went on looking through the tin. "We always wondered who'd dig it up," he said, "but I'd forgotten all about it – for years now. Forgotten all about it ..." His eyes grew moist as he picked out the penknife. "This was mine and all. It was Eric who busted it – trying to carve a caveman on the cave wall ..."

Kipper fished the broken stub of pencil out of his pocket. "Could we have your autograph?" he asked simply.

Mr Foster had just managed to light the camp fire for the potato-bake. He stood up, dusting ash and wood splinters off himself, and blew his whistle. First-years came stampeding from every corner of the field. Last to arrive, and most out of breath, were Mackenzie and his friends.

They were clutching the tin which they had unearthed in the cave. Mr Foster eyed it impatiently.

"What have you been doing with that thing, taking it for a walk? Put it in your tent and go and wash. You boys look as if you've been playing in a compost heap!"

He wondered why they ran off laughing.

When Kipper returned, with most of the grime removed from his person, hands in pockets and whistling loudly, Quentin Parslow and Nigel Bailey eyed him with apprehension. But Kipper just strolled nonchalantly past them, with the rest of the Co.

"Wasn't it amazing, us meeting one of the original Cavemen like that?" he observed loudly.

"And we never would've, if our tin hadn't got pinched," agreed Andrew equally loudly.

"And he told us what some of the other Cavemen are doing now," said Rasheeda. "Imagine, one of 'em growing up to be a teacher!"

"I thought it was *really* interesting when he said Eric's working in Australia," commented Andrew, "And there's one of 'em on an oil rig. Best thing that could've happened, us meeting him like that, *which* we wouldn't't've if our tin hadn't got pinched."

"And this souvenir he gave us is definitely the best thing we've got for our time capsule, isn't it, Kipper?" added Rasheeda, waving a sheet from a police notebook with *Arthur* written on it.

Quentin Parslow thrust his sharp face close to Kipper's.

"You've been off camp," he hissed triumphantly. "I'm *telling* on you!"

He turned towards Mr Foster.

"Of course," Kipper mused, "what I don't understand is how those boys – Willis's cousin and that mob – *knew* which tent was ours, Andrew. After all, no one could have *told* them, could they? Not after old Tandy had warned us not to have anything to do with 'em."

Quentin Parslow stopped in his tracks.

"Good point," agreed Rasheeda. "I mean, if someone *did* tell 'em which tent was yours, they'd be in mega-big trouble, wouldn't they? *Especially* if they just happened to have been there when old Tandy warned us."

Kipper nodded his head. "They would, Sheed. They would," he prophesied.

Quentin Parslow slumped down on the grass beside Nigel Bailey. Their glowering, sullen expressions spoke volumes.

It seemed to them that Mackenzie and his rabble were getting far too much glory.

Things were going to change. Quentin Parslow resolved to see to that, at the very first opportunity.

8

Quentin's Revenge

THE following day the group transferred back to their hostel, stopping *en route*, to Kipper's disgust, to visit the museum. Trust old Fossil-face not to let them off being educated even for one day. Kipper and Co. trudged round the exhibits with expressions of deep boredom.

"When do we get to the good stuff?" Andrew wanted to know. "The canoeing and raft-building?"

"Friday," said Mr Foster, crisply, overhearing. "The last day. And not then, if you don't stop trying to trip each other up when you think I'm not looking, lad."

Kipper and Andrew suspected this was an idle threat, but they stopped, just in case. The canoeing and raft-building promised to be the best events of the entire week, and they didn't intend to risk missing them.

But then on Thursday came the visit to the fire station, and that's when all the trouble started.

The fire station itself was not the cause; it was good fun there. By the time Kipper had tried on a fireman's breathing apparatus, slid down the firemen's pole (once with permission and twice more without) and been dragged off the side of a fire-engine by Mr Foster, he had once again changed his ideas about his future career. Being a fireman must be dead brilliant, he decided; hurtling along crowded roads in a fire-engine, siren whooping and lights flashing, making everything else dodge out of your way, and then getting to put on the breathing apparatus and squirt water everywhere.

In the Fire Display Room, where photos of fire damage were on display, the Chief Fire Officer gave the first-formers a lecture on fire safety. He demonstrated a fire-man's lift, and showed them what to do if they were ever in a burning building. Kipper listened keenly, for once. It would all come in very useful for when he was a fireman.

Then the Chief Fire Officer picked up a damp towel from a basin.

"If you're caught in a smoke-filled room, remember the air at floor-level is the freshest, because smoke rises. So drop to the floor. If at all possible, place a damp towel over your nose and mouth . . . like this . . ."

Kipper looked interested. There was a good game here.

That evening, at the hostel, while the others played in the games room or watched TV in the lounge, Kipper and Co. slipped upstairs to one of the bathrooms, half-filled the bath with water and tipped their face-towels into it.

They crawled happily up and down the corridors, hold-ing the soaking, dripping towels to their noses and mouths, and coughing and spluttering dramatically in the billowing clouds of imaginary smoke. Then Rasheeda had the bright idea of using their bath towels, which, being bigger, could be tied around their heads, leaving their hands free for crawling; so they tipped these into the bath as well, and resumed crawling, leaving bigger trails of water behind them.

They were so engrossed in their game that they didn't notice Quentin Parslow creeping into the bathroom, and out again.

"Right," Kipper instructed them, rising dripping from the floor, "now I'm the fireman come to rescue you." He dropped his towel and grabbed hold of Andrew round the neck. Andrew gurgled, and his coughs became louder and more genuine. He waved his arms wildly and yanked his towel free of his mouth.

"Get off, you great prawn! You're strangling me!" he complained, spluttering.

"I'm just pulling you up so I can do that fireman's lift on you like they showed us. I can't lift you when you're crawling, can I? Now shut up so I can save you. *Hey!*"

Andrew's towel caught him on the side of the head with a wet smack. Vengefully Kipper snatched up his own towel again, and the fight was on.

The twins waded in happily, swinging their own wet towels, smacking at each other. Large damp patches and spray marks began to appear on the walls. The Co. shrieked and yelled and swiped, and the faint, trickling sounds from the bathroom went unheard.

Suddenly Quentin Parslow's shrill, virtuous voice pierced the air.

"*Look! I said* you ought to see what they're doing, Miss!"

Kipper and Co. spun round. Mrs Tandy was standing there, frowning, her arms folded. Kipper assumed his innocent look.

"What," enquired Mrs Tandy coldly, "is the meaning of this?"

Kipper turned the look up to full strength. "We were just practising what they showed us, Miss. In case of fire. We..."

He was interrupted by a squeal of well-simulated alarm from Quentin Parslow.

"Ooh, *Miss*! Look what they've done to the bathroom *floor*!"

They all looked. Kipper, Andrew and the twins gasped aloud.

Mrs Tandy shrieked beside them. "CHRISTOPHER!"

The bath taps were running. Water was trickling over the side of the tub. The floor was already flooded to a depth of two centimetres.

Mrs Tandy splashed through the water and turned off the taps, then rounded on Kipper and Co. There was no innocence on their faces now, just looks of the deepest bewilderment and horror.

"All of you – clean this up – RIGHT NOW!" she snapped.

Kipper found his voice. "B-but, Miss! We didn't do that! We turned the taps off, Miss ... we ..." His voice faded away. He just couldn't understand it. He *knew* he'd turned off the taps. How had this happened? *How*?

And then he saw Quentin Parslow smirking triumphantly behind Mrs Tandy's back, and he knew *just* how it had happened.

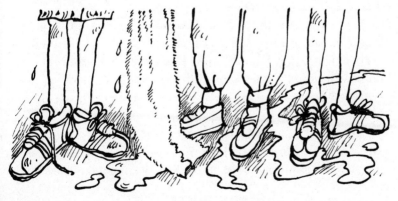

97

He gritted his teeth and turned dull red as Mrs Tandy's tongue went into action. She gave them a short, sharp talking-to, and then she slapped cloths into their hands and got down on her knees to assist in mopping up the water.

When the flood had been reduced to several small puddles, she straightened up and drew a deep breath.

"You will finish cleaning up in here, and then you will report to the teachers' lounge. By that time Mr Foster and I will have decided what is to be done with you. Now I'm going to report this to the hostel manager, and assure her that you will be punished. If there is any water damage, and they charge us, the bill will go straight to your parents!"

She left them. Maya was sniffling. She wiped her eyes on her already damp sleeve.

"How did it happen?" demanded Rasheeda. "Did we leave a tap on?"

"No, we didn't," said Kipper bitterly. "Want three guesses?" He raised his voice in a good imitation of Quentin Parslow's nasal tones. "Ooh, Miss, look what they've done to the floor."

"We'll get him," said Andrew through his teeth.

"It's no good," Maya gulped. "If it was him, we can't prove it. And anyway, we're in enough trouble already."

Nervously, with dragging steps and heavy hearts they made their way to the teachers' lounge.

Mr Foster was in his chair, smoking his pipe and watching TV. He had his back to them, and he did not immediately turn around. Kipper knew this technique, and his heart sank still further. The wait-and-let-them-sweat bit – it was a trick Mr Foster used only when you were in the direst of dire trouble.

Then, very slowly, Mr Foster leaned forward to switch the TV off. He stubbed his pipe out in the ashtray, and tipped the contents into a wicker wastepaper-basket by

his chair. Only then did he turn to face them. They quailed at his expression. When he spoke, his tone was icy.

"I have given up trying to work out why you four do anything you do," he said softly. "In five days, you have risked your necks – and other people's – clambering about on cliffs when expressly forbidden to; you have trespassed in a private castle playing some silly game of murderers . . ."

Kipper opened his mouth to defend himself. Mr Foster rose meaningfully from his chair. He seemed to have grown about half a metre taller. Kipper gulped, and closed his mouth again quickly.

"And now, not content with being the biggest little idiots in the first year, you have to go and flood a bathroom. The manager tells me she has inspected the ceiling of the room below, and you may consider yourselves very lucky that no damage appears to have been done."

The Co. breathed again, and exchanged expressions of relief.

"And for your punishment," continued Mr Foster, "you will all stay in tomorrow and write out five hundred times: 'I must learn not to behave like a stupid little idiot'. And you will hand the lines to me when I get back from tomorrow's activities."

This took half a second to sink in. Then the Co.'s eyes jerked open in shock.

"B–but, sir!" Kipper protested in agony. "Not tomorrow, sir – it's the canoeing! And the raft-building! Please, sir . . ."

"BE QUIET!" shouted Mr Foster in a voice that shook the room. "Now go to your rooms – and STAY THERE!"

Quentin Parslow, who had been listening outside the door, scurried away, grinning. His plan had succeeded better than he'd dared hope.

Miserably, the Co. went to their rooms.

"If there's no real damage, why're they being so grotty?" Rasheeda complained.

Maya summoned up all the optimism she could muster. "Oh, well, maybe by tomorrow he'll have simmered down a bit," she suggested hopefully. "Perhaps he'll change his mind."

Andrew snorted. "Yeah. And maybe Parslow'll come clean and confess. I *don't* think!"

There was indeed to be no reprieve for them. Next morning, Mr Foster, his face set and stern, marched them to the common room and sat them down at the table with pens and paper. Miss Lambe, only too relieved to be excused the canoeing and raft-building, sat in the room

with them, in an easy-chair; and Kipper and Co. were forced to watch through the window as the coach drove away carrying Mr Foster, Mrs Tandy and all the rest of the first years to a nearby river, and the waiting canoes.

Quentin Parslow gave them a triumphant wave from the coach as it passed their window. Pure fury rose in Kipper's heart. He jabbed the table with his biro so hard that the point left a small, deep, dark-blue hole in the polished surface.

"Hope he *sinks*," he muttered.

"Come along, now," said Miss Lambe, not unkindly. "You must get on with your lines. Mr Foster will want to see them all finished when he gets back."

She settled comfortably in her chair, picked up a paperback book, and began to read.

Kipper stabbed the table again, glowering. Next to him, Andrew was half-heartedly trying to push a small spider into a crack in the table. Rasheeda was staring blankly out of the window, her cheek cupped in her hand. Only Maya took up her pen and began slowly to write, a tear trickling down the side of her nose.

Time dragged by. At last Rasheeda and then Andrew picked up their pens too, although all Andrew used his for was to punch holes all round the edges of his sheet of paper. Kipper was scowling out of the window, deep in planning the revenge he was going to wreak on Parslow, just as soon as he could get his hands on him.

But even that was little comfort. The fact remained that right now Quentin Parslow was enjoying a day's canoeing and raft-building, and he and the gang were stuck here, being punished for something that for once they hadn't done.

If only old Woolley Lambe wasn't there, at least they could do something with the day. He knew that a football was kept in the common room cupboard. If only she wasn't keeping a beady eye on them . . .

He glanced at her and realised, with a little lifting of his spirits, that she wasn't. Her beady eyes were closed.

He nudged Andrew and, finger to his lips, jerked his head towards Miss Lambe. Andrew looked, and leaned

across the table to poke Rasheeda, who in her turn nudged Maya.

Miss Lambe's mouth was open, her breathing soft and regular, her book lying face downwards in her lap. The comfort of the chair, the peaceful silence of the morning after a week of constant cheerful noise and chatter, had lulled her gently into a pleasant, dreamless sleep.

The frown on Kipper's freckled countenance cleared. He rose and crept silently to the cupboard. Then, the football tucked under his arm, he gestured to the Co. to follow, and tiptoed out of the room.

Once they were all safely outside the building, Kipper stretched.

"I'm not staying in there writing those rotten lines. Come on, let's go and play two-a-side!"

They sprinted for the field behind the hostel, feeling happier. This was better than being stuck inside doing an unjust punishment. Dividing into two teams, Kipper and Maya versus Andrew and Rasheeda, they settled into a vigorous game.

In the common room, Miss Lambe slumbered contentedly. There was no one to disturb her, for the hostel cleaners were not on duty that day. It was cook's day off too, for the guests were to have a barbecue that evening. The only other person in the building, besides Miss Lambe, was the manager, who was working quietly on the accounts in her office. Everything in the hostel was peaceful.

And upstairs, in the teachers' lounge, a curl of smoke began to rise from the back of the dormant TV set.

9

Fire Alarm

THE game was beginning to go in favour of Kipper and Maya, when suddenly Rasheeda missed saving a goal kick from Kipper and gave a scream. She was staring at the hostel.

"LOOK!"

"Don't try making excuses," said Kipper sternly. "You flubbed that one. That's 13–11 to us –"

"FIRE!" screamed Rasheeda.

They looked.

Black smoke was wreathing from an upstairs window of the hostel.

"Oh, no," whispered Maya.

"What do we *do*?" gasped Andrew.

Kipper became business-like. "What the fire bloke said. Get everyone out of the building, and ring the Fire-Brigade."

"Cor, yeah!" Andrew enthused. "Bags I smash the fire-alarm thing."

"All right," Kipper agreed magnanimously. "But I'm doing the ringing the Fire-Brigade bit. Come on!"

They rushed back to the hostel.

There was no sign of any smoke or flames downstairs, except for a faint smell that was worse than Mr Foster's pipe on a bad day. The twins ran into the common room.

"Miss Lambe! FIRE!" they shouted.

Miss Lambe awoke groggily. It took her a moment to come to her senses. Then she turned pale.

"What? Oh, my goodness . . . Oh, dear!"

She stumbled out of her chair just as a shrill, jangling noise pierced the air.

In the hallway, by the main entrance, Andrew stood by the shattered glass of the fire-alarm on the wall.

"They said at the station to smash 'em with your shoe to set 'em off," he reported proudly, "but you could whack 'em with a trainer till the cows come home and it wouldn't bust, so I got this stone off the drive –"

"Get outside!" screamed Miss Lambe, hastening him and the twins to the front door.

The manager came hurrying out, demanding to know who was messing about with the fire-alarm. Her expression changed when she, too, smelt the smoke.

She went a few steps up the stairs and returned, looking shaken. "It's the lounge upstairs . . . there's smoke coming under the door . . . ."

"That's the teachers' lounge!" said Rasheeda. "Lucky you weren't in there, isn't it, Miss?"

Miss Lambe did not hear her. She was looking around wildly.

"Christopher! Where's Christopher?"

Andrew pointed back inside. "Ringing the Fire-Brigade."

Kipper was on the phone in the hallway. "You'd better tell 'em to hurry up," he was saying firmly. "I'm telling you, it's burning down . . . well, the top bit of it is, any-

way . . ." He paused. "No, I'm *not*," he said indignantly. "It's *real*! And you'd just better . . ."

Miss Lambe hurried up to him and took the phone. "Go outside at once, Christopher, and stay there! Oh, dear oh dear . . . This is Miss Lambe of Rexley Manor School," she said into the receiver. "Yes, the fire appears to be on the upper floor. *Do* please hurry."

Kipper was fuming as he joined his friends in the driveway. "They didn't believe me! Thought I was mucking about . . . Huh!"

The emergency services must have believed Miss Lambe, however, for less than five minutes later the Co. heard the distant wail of a siren, and then a fire-engine raced up the driveway, its blue lights flashing, its siren dying down as it screeched to a halt in a spray of gravel.

Their old friend the Chief Fire Officer was first out.

"Anyone in there?" he asked.

The manager said there were no hostel employees in the building, and Miss Lambe, who had just counted Kipper, Andrew and the twins for the third time to reassure herself that they were all safe, assured the Chief Fire Officer that there were no school children left inside either.

The manager showed one of the firemen to the nearest water hydrant, and then hoses were unravelled and a couple of firemen raced into the hostel.

Kipper and Co. watched, enthralled. This was by far the biggest excitement of the holiday. Seeing real, live firemen putting out a real, live fire close to . . . Beside it, even the joys of canoeing and raft-building began to pale.

Meanwhile, on the riverbank, Quentin Parslow and Nigel Bailey were feeling pretty proud of themselves. They had just been shown by the instructor how to lash logs together to construct their raft, and they had already mastered the technique and earned themselves a few words of praise. Their heads swelled visibly.

"Hope old Mackenzie's enjoying doing his lines," smirked Nigel Bailey.

Quentin Parslow grinned, nastily. "Well, he wouldn't have enjoyed *this*, anyway," he observed, jerking a thumb towards the river where some of the others were already in canoes. "He had enough of *water* yesterday!"

Nigel Bailey giggled. "Wish I'd seen it, Quent. Brilliant idea of yours, that taps bit."

"Telling me! Pass that other bit of twine. Yeah, shows how thick Mackenzie is. He's thicker than these logs. He never sees me going into the bathroom, right? And he never hears the water flowing. Shows you how thick –"

His friend's sudden sharp warning nudge in the ribs came too late. Quentin Parslow looked round and up to see Mrs Tandy standing behind him.

His jaw opened slackly at the expression on her face.

Back at the hostel, the fire was out. It had been caught before it spread to any other room; and, to the Co.'s delight, they were allowed to go up with the Chief Fire Officer and, under strict supervision, have a look at the charred and smoke-blackened teachers' lounge.

It was a mess. The television set had been reduced to

a heap of twisted metal; most of the easy-chairs had been destroyed, and the few that still stood had black, scorched holes in their upholstery. The walls were grimy with soot and the floor was squelchy with water. The smell of smoke and burned foam-filled furniture was everywhere.

Rasheeda wrinkled her nose. "What a pong," she announced.

"It could have been far worse," said the Fire Officer, as they descended the stairs. "Left any longer, the fire would have spread for certain. It's lucky you young 'uns spotted it when you did."

"What started it?" asked Andrew.

"The TV set. Easy to tell. That was where the fire was centred, and it certainly seems to have sustained the most damage."

Kipper whistled.

"My gran had a set that caught fire once," said Andrew. "While she was watching the wrestling, smoke started coming out of it, she said."

"It can happen," the Fire Officer agreed. "Old set, left plugged in. Well, you four promise me now that you'll stay well clear of that room, all right?"

They promised, and he went off to talk to the manager.

As he left, to the astonishment of Kipper and Co., the school coach turned in at the gates, and out stepped Mrs Tandy, her hand on the shoulder of a sullen Quentin Parslow.

"Whatever is a fire-engine doing here?" she demanded.

With a flushed face, her hands still shaking from the excitement of it all, Miss Lambe told her the whole story.

"And these four were *so* brave!" she cried, flinging an arm around Andrew, who happened to be the nearest. "They did *all* the right things! They cleared the building, and set off the alarm, and called the Fire-Brigade!"

Andrew wriggled free and moved hastily out of hugging range. Kipper shot a glance at Quentin Parslow, whose

mouth was hanging open in amazement and envy.

"If they hadn't been here," cried Miss Lambe, clasping her hands, "the hostel could have burned to the ground."

A sour expression descended over Quentin Parslow's features. That morning's taste of victory was beginning to turn very sour in his mouth.

Mrs Tandy was giving Kipper a searching look. "How did you know a room upstairs at the back was on fire," she enquired, "when you were downstairs in the front?"

Kipper had been expecting this question. "We sort of smelled smoke," he explained blandly. Well, it wasn't far from the truth. He *had* smelled smoke. He hadn't said when, had he?

"Hmm," said Mrs Tandy. "I don't think I'll go into that one too closely. Particularly as the lines you were supposed to be writing do not appear to have been fully deserved."

It was the turn of Kipper and Co. to be surprised. Mrs Tandy gave Quentin Parslow a little push forward, and the bitter scowl descended over his sharp features again. "This young man has . . . *confessed* everything," she said. "He switched on the taps that flooded the bathroom. You four should not have been playing with wet towels in the first place; but missing part of this morning's activities can count as sufficient punishment for that. Quentin will

stay here in your place and write the five hundred lines.
You four can come back to the river with me."

Loud yells of delight greeted this statement. Quentin
Parslow's face grew darker red.

"And for keeping quiet and letting these four take the
blame, Quentin," continued Mrs Tandy, "you will not
be attending tonight's disco either. In you go."

Miss Lambe escorted the glowering Quentin back into
the hostel while Kipper, Andrew and the twins piled
joyously on to the coach.

Mr Foster was waiting for them at the river, where all
their companions could be seen splashing about merrily
in canoes. He greeted them sternly.

"I hope you four have learned your lesson . . ." he began.

Mrs Tandy interrupted, and told him all about the fire.
Mr Foster started violently when she mentioned that it
had been in the teachers' lounge. A keen observer might
have noticed his face turning slightly pale.

"Good Lord! And these four . . . they actually . . . Good
Lord!"

He stared at Kipper and Co. He seemed to be finding
it difficult to speak.

"Well," he said at last in a strangely shaken voice, "you did the right thing. I shall – I shall be making a far pleasanter report to the Headmaster than – than I thought necessary. In fact, I – I see no need to report any of your – activities to him at all . . . Well done."

He left them speechless.

"Phew!" said Rasheeda, at last.

"I thought he'd *do* us for skiving off doing those lines," muttered Andrew. "He *must've* guessed we'd skived, else how did we see the fire? Old Tandy worked it out."

Kipper shook his head. He, too, had been expecting something other than just puzzled congratulations from old Fossil-face. And there had been something so odd about his attitude just now . . . something weird, ashamed almost . . . He didn't understand it.

"Maybe he's sorry he punished us unfairly," suggested Maya.

Kipper shook his head again. In his view, teachers frequently punished them unfairly, and seldom seemed to suffer any pangs of conscience about it.

He turned to see the two canoes on the river bank, with the instructor standing beside them, and his face cleared. Who could figure out teachers – but then with canoes, a river and a glorious day at your disposal, who'd bother to waste time trying?

The rest of the day was brilliant. They learned to paddle a canoe backwards and forwards, how to roll over, go underwater and then right the canoe again. They held an impromptu canoe race which Kipper won, and Rasheeda lost her paddle in some reeds and nearly fell in trying to retrieve it.

During the picnic lunch, they regaled their impressed and envious companions with the tale of the fire; and after lunch, to crown the day, they were all four given a special lesson in raft-building to make up for the one they had missed. They constructed a small raft which held together long enough for Kipper to paddle it out triumphantly into mid-stream, where it slowly and gracefully tipped up and deposited him in the water before floating apart, to the loud hilarity of his friends.

All the way back to the hostel, they argued energetically about whose log-lashing and knot-tying had been most at fault. All the other first-formers were in good voice too, discussing the events of the day and looking forward to seeing what was left of the hostel – Kipper's dramatic description of the fire had slightly exaggerated its size and ferocity.

The only two silent travellers on the coach were Nigel Bailey, who knew that he was going to get it from Quentin Parslow for starting that conversation about the taps, and Mr Foster, who for some reason had a troubled expression on his face.

He disappeared up to the roped-off teachers' lounge as soon as they got back, and then could be seen with an even longer face going into the manager's office to make a private phone call. He emerged from this looking even more troubled, tapping his empty pipe thoughtfully on the palm of one hand.

That evening came the final barbecue and disco. Mr Foster, who was in charge of the barbecue, said not a word as he piled eagerly-proffered plates high with chicken drumsticks, sausages, lamb chops and onion rings. Maya noticed with concern that he ate nothing himself.

"Maybe he's not feeling well?" she suggested.

"Could be the thought of the disco coming up," Rasheeda proposed. "Old people never do like decent music."

Maya nudged her quickly, for Miss Lambe and Mrs Tandy were passing.

"Well," Mrs Tandy was saying, "I *did* warn him about that pipe of his. He *would* knock the ashes out in the wicker wastepaper-basket."

"I must say I did rather dislike his smoking in the lounge," Miss Lambe agreed meekly. "His tobacco *did* smell rather . . . pungent."

"Apparently his wife can't stand it either," said Mrs Tandy. "He told me he's banned from smoking at home except in his study. I don't blame her!" She laughed, then sighed. "Poor old Bob, though. He must be feeling pretty bad now."

They walked on. Kipper whistled, and snapped his fingers.

"Hey, that's it! That's what's bugging old Fossil-face. He thinks *he* started that fire!"

"But he didn't!" cried Maya. "The firemen said it was the TV! He's blaming himself for something he didn't do!"

"Makes a change from him blaming *us* for something

we didn't do," said Rasheeda, but she spoke without conviction.

They looked at Mr Foster. He was leaning against a tree, and his face seemed gloomier than ever in the fading evening light.

"Oh, come on," said Kipper.

He approached Mr Foster. The others followed.

"Sir?" said Kipper.

Mr Foster started. He had been frowning into the distance and had not noticed them coming. "What?"

"I didn't know TV sets could suddenly do that, did you, sir?"

Mr Foster sighed. What was the boy going on about now? "Pardon, Mackenzie?"

"The TV set, sir. In the lounge. It burst into flames, sir. VHOOOM! Just went straight up. That's what started the fire."

Mr Foster's attention was suddenly riveted on him.

"*What* did you say? A *television* started it?"

"Yes, sir."

"It was an old set, sir."

"My gran had one that went up in smoke too."

"Who told you that?" asked Mr Foster sharply.

"My gran did, sir. She was halfway through the wrestling –"

"No, no, *no*! The fire *here*. Who told you it was started by the TV set?"

"The Chief Fire bloke," explained Kipper.

Mr Foster's whole body relaxed. His face cleared.

"I see! Well, well." He heaved a deep sigh, and straightened up. "Well, thank you. Thank you for telling me."

"Just thought you'd be interested, sir."

"Yes, indeed, I most certainly ... Oh, *no*!" Mr Foster broke off with a wild exclamation and smacked his forehead with the palm of his hand. "Blast it! I've just rung my wife and told her ... I promised her I'd give up smoking because I thought ... Oh, *blast* it!"

"You did, sir?"

"Yes, I did! Honestly, boy, couldn't you have told me *earlier*?"

He stomped off, leaving Kipper and Co. staring at each other.

"*Grown-ups*," said Kipper with feeling. "I'm *never* going to understand 'em."

10

The Time Capsule

NEXT morning after breakfast Kipper and Co. collected the large empty biscuit-tin from Mrs Tandy. Proudly they laid out the souvenirs which they had collected on Kipper's bed.

There was the Sudbury Castle notebook and pen, the guide-book signed by Lord Sudbury; one of the knights in armour – Rasheeda's, which the twins donated, explaining that that still left one between them; and there was the page of the police notebook with Arthur's signature.

There was a knock at the door and Mrs Tandy came in, smiling.

"Here are the photos," she said, and handed them the pictures she had taken just before they went to Sudbury Castle. There was the one of the four of them, on the back of which they wrote their names, and the one the coach driver had taken of the whole group and the staff. On the back of this, Maya wrote simply "The first year, Rexley Manor Comprehensive".

"You ought to write everyone's names on the back," Mrs Tandy suggested.

"We got everyone to write their names in our notebook," said Maya shyly, "so they'll all have a part of themselves in our capsule."

"Except for two who wouldn't sign," murmured Rasheeda.

There was another knock. This time it was Mr Foster, clutching a brand-new *Beano* comic.

"As they had one in the original tin . . ." he explained.

The Co. were touched.

"Cor, thanks, sir!"

"Brilliant!"

"Bob," murmured Mrs Tandy.

Mr Foster pretended not to hear her.

"Right, it's just straight down to the beach, bury the tin, and then we're coming straight back. The coach leaves here at ten-thirty . . ."

"Mr Foster," said Mrs Tandy mock-sternly, "that was *not* the souvenir you were going to contribute, now *was* it?"

For a moment, Mr Foster tried an innocent expression that would have done credit to Kipper himself. Then he caught Mrs Tandy's eye, sighed and surrendered.

"Oh, all right," he conceded regretfully.

He fished in his jacket-pocket, and handed over his pipe.

"Go on, take it," he said ruefully. "I *did* promise to give up. No doubt my wife will be eternally grateful to you!"

Mrs Tandy chuckled.

"Right, down to the beach. Come on!"

All the first-years who wanted to watch the burying of the time capsule had gathered outside, chattering excitedly. There were twenty-six of them; and if the only pair who had refused to sign their names in the book had also chosen to absent themselves from this ceremony, nobody missed them.

Mr Foster, carrying a spade which the hostel manager had kindly lent him, rounded them up, and they set off for the beach. Kipper was carrying the old Cavemen tin and Andrew and the twins took it in turns to carry the new one.

Outside the hostel gates, a tall, portly figure in blue was waiting for them. He smiled, coughed and held out an envelope.

"You told me you'd be burying your tin this morning, just before you left. I thought you might like these to put in it."

Kipper opened the envelope and took out two photos. One was of Arthur himself, in his uniform, and the other showed a tall, tanned, balding man, standing by a barbecue, on a beach of very golden sand, with a deep-blue sea behind him. Kipper did not need to turn the photo over and read the name on the back, to guess who this was.

"Eric," he said. "In Australia."

"Yes, well," said P.C. Arthur with another cough, his red cheeks growing slightly redder. "I just thought . . . link with the past and all that . . . seeing as you're burying our tin again this morning and yours with it, and what-have-you . . ."

"Why don't you come and help us?" asked Rasheeda.

Arthur brightened. "Well, now, if I wouldn't be in

118

anyone's way . . ."

He accompanied them happily down to the beach. The
tide was far out this morning. The first-years assembled
on the sands below the cave, and Kipper opened the new
Cavemen tin for the last time, put in Arthur's envelope,
and took out the Sudbury Castle notebook, which he
handed to Maya. As their companions clustered round to
look at the contents of the time capsule before it was buried
for posterity, Maya was ushered to the front of the group,
and Mrs Tandy clapped her hands for silence.

"Go on, Maya," she said encouragingly.

Shyly, Maya began to read aloud the entries she had
made in the notebook.

"Our Holiday.

*"We came here for a week. Kipper and Andrew found the
tin, we call it the Cavemen tin because the Cavemen were in
it so we thuoght we would do one to, like a time capseule. Kipper
and Andrew had to be rescued by a fishing-boat, they were called
Dave and Bill. A helicopter saved Mr Foster, everyone could
of drowned because the tide came up.*

"At Sudbury Castle Kipper caught some thieves who were

stealing jewls but there wasn't a murdur. He gave us a guide-book and the night in armour, he wasn't going to murdur Lord Sudbury because he was him and it was a pajint."

The Co. nodded their approval. Only Arthur was looking slightly puzzled. Maya cleared her throat and read on.

"Then we went camping. Willis told his cousin we were here so he stoal our tin, but we got it back . . ."

"What's all this?" said Mr Foster sharply.

Kipper groaned under his breath. He'd forgotten to warn Maya not to read that bit aloud. But P.C. Arthur came to his rescue.

"I was in on that one, sir. No trouble. All above board," he assured him.

"Ye gods," muttered Mr Foster. "They've got police protection now!" He looked hard at Kipper. "Well," he said at length, "perhaps I don't want to ask about it at this late stage . . . Read on, Maya."

Maya obliged.

"We met Arther, he was the littlest caveman he is a policman now. We got his ortograph. The leader was his brother Eric, he is in Australea now.

"The hostel almost burned down, but the fire brigaid came. It was the TV that burst into flames, not Mr Foster after all."

"I'm very glad to hear it," murmured Mrs Tandy.

"We saw them put it out we had been to the fire stashun. We went canooing and lots of other things it was ace. Now we are going back to Rexley Manor School, it is in Leatherham, altho Kipper Andrew Rasheeda and me live in Rexley Green. We want to come again next year it was brilliunt. Maya Chand."

"Well," observed Mrs Tandy, as Arthur led a brief round of applause, "whenever did you write all that?"

"She did a bit most evenings," said Rasheeda.

Maya handed the book back to Kipper, who placed it in the tin and closed the lid firmly. Then he, Andrew, and the twins began to climb up to the cave, taking Mr Foster and the shovel with them.

Halfway up, Kipper turned to Arthur. "Coming?" he said simply.

Arthur came.

With the spade, it was the work of a very few minutes on Mr Foster's part to dig a hole deep enough to take both tins. Then Kipper handed Arthur the old Cavemen tin, and Arthur knelt to place it in the hole, before Kipper placed their own tin on the top. Then everyone took a turn at shovelling the sand back into the hole; and, when the tins were buried, Kipper and Andrew rearranged the flat white marker stones on top, just as they had found them.

Arthur's eyes were moist. "Well, I never," he said. "All those years . . . feels like it was yesterday . . . Well, I never. Who'd have thought, eh?" He turned aside and blew his nose.

Once outside the cave, Mr Foster straightened up with relief. It hadn't been easy, digging in a bent-over position.

"Right," he said. "Everyone back to the hostel and load up the coach!"

The first-years were already scuffling their way across the sands. Kipper and Co. hung back to say goodbye to P.C. Arthur.

"You going to tell Eric about this?" asked Andrew.

"Already written to him, after I met you the other day," said Arthur. "I'll have to write again now, and tell him about this bit. Well, take care, all."

He raised a hand to them as they hurried off after their companions. He was the only one who saw Kipper, in the rear, suddenly stop, glance surreptitiously around, bend down and transfer something from a rockpool into his pocket.

Half an hour later, still talking at full volume, the thirty-two first-years of Rexley Manor piled on to their coach for the long journey home. Mr Foster, standing by the coach door with a check list to tick off names, overheard the conversation of Kipper and Co.

"Just think," Rasheeda was saying, "in years' and years' time, someone'll dig that lot up and then they'll know all about us."

Mr Foster raised his eyes heavenwards.

"Yeah," Andrew agreed. "By that time, I'm going to be a fireman."

"Yeah, me too. And fly helicopters and do coastguard rescues."

"You can't do 'em all!"

"All right then, I'll be a fireman for a year, and then fly helicopters for a year . . ."

"Or you could be one in the week, and do the other

one at weekends . . . flying the helicopter, say. I bet more people need rescuing at weekends . . ."

Their voices died away as they stampeded on to the coach, to be replaced by other equally strident voices whose owners were all just as keen on getting the back seat. Mr Foster climbed aboard, sank on to one of the front seats, and sighed.

"It's only been a week," he muttered. "I can't *believe* what those four can get up to in one week."

Mrs Tandy hid a smile. It *was* Mr Foster's first full day without his pipe . . .

"Courage, Bob," she murmured. "Only three hours to go, and we hand them back to their parents."

"Thank Heaven," said Mr Foster with feeling. "Only three more hours. Even Christopher Mackenzie can't possibly get up to any more of his shenanigans in three hours on a coach!" He looked at Mrs Tandy. "Can he?" he appealed.

In the second-to-rear seat, Quentin Parslow turned round and stuck his tongue out at Kipper, then turned to face front, smirking.

And in the back seat, Kipper quietly removed from his knapsack the large and by now very irritable shore-crab which he had taken from the rockpool.

He leaned forward stealthily.

Seconds later, the air was shattered by a piercing yell.

Mr Foster leapt up and made his way down the aisle between the rows of giggling pupils, to where Quentin Parslow was hopping up and down, shrieking and clutching frantically at the back of his T-shirt.

Kipper and Co. exchanged quick, satisfied grins before switching on their expressions of innocence.

"Us, sir?" they said, as a large, angry crab dropped out of the back of Quentin Parslow's shirt and scuttled under one of the seats.

Mr Foster closed his eyes in silent agony. Three hours, it appeared, was plenty of time for Christopher Mackenzie and his crew to strike again.